DON'T INT
MOMMY

50¢

"Jessica Ann!"

Both Mommy and Jessi_____ _____ of the voice emanating fr___ ___ very nearby open door where, from within the library, Mrs. Jensen, Head Librarian at Central Middle School, leaned out with a stern expression.

"Where's your next class?" the teacher demanded curtly. She was a usually pleasant-looking woman in her early forties, but her expression right now was anything but pleasant.

"F-first floor, west wing," Jessica Ann managed.

"Then you better get a move on." The teacher eyed the girl's mother, who had withdrawn into a corner like a child being punished. "You're Mrs. Sterling, aren't you? You're not supposed to be seeing your daughter—"

Jessica Ann touched the teacher's arm lightly; the girl's head was back and her eyes narrow as she cautioned, "I wouldn't do that if I were you...."

Other *Leisure* books by Max Allan Collins:
MOMMY

Mommy's Day

Max Allan Collins

LEISURE BOOKS      NEW YORK CITY

For Steven Henke—
Mommy's "midwife"

A LEISURE BOOK®

May 1998

Published by

Dorchester Publishing Co., Inc.
276 Fifth Avenue
New York, NY 10001

If you purchased this book without a cover you should be aware that this book is stolen property. It was reported as "unsold and destroyed" to the publisher and neither the author nor the publisher has received any payment for this "stripped book."

Copyright © 1998 by Max Allan Collins

All rights reserved. No part of this book may be reproduced or transmitted in any form or by any electronic or mechanical means, including photocopying, recording or by any information storage and retrieval system, without the written permission of the Publisher, except where permitted by law.

ISBN 0-8439-4386-6

The name "Leisure Books" and the stylized "L" with design are trademarks of Dorchester Publishing Co., Inc.

Printed in the United States of America.

"Her mind no longer moved in the straight line of rational thought; it turned like a rotating wheel, in rapid, intense circles of emotion which she seemed unable to escape...."

—William March

mommy's day

ONE:

A Child's Prayer

Chapter One

On the day Jessica Ann Sterling's mommy was to die, the sun dappled the Mississippi River under a sky as blue as her mother's eyes. The fluffy white clouds seemed to take the sting out of the bright sunshine, leaving the tree-shaded streets of Ferndale, on the Iowa side of the river, washed in a golden glow. On a spring day like this, the little industrial town seemed as peaceful as a vintage postcard, at least as long as you stayed away from certain parts of it.

When they would drive places, her mommy used to avoid "the inner city," which was filled with "Mexicans and poor white trash"; her beautiful mother's patrician features would tighten as she uttered such pronouncements, her lovely upper lip curling into the faintest sneer. Jessica

Ann's aunt Beth, her face (eyes especially) filled with compassion, referred to these same people as "underprivileged," and her new uncle Paul called them "disenfranchised," but the twelve-year-old had noticed that her uncle and aunt seemed to avoid that part of town, too.

Beth had told the child she could skip Saturday morning choir practice, "considering." *Considering my mother's being murdered today*, the child had thought, but kept it to herself; she had been well trained by her mother not to be snippy.

But Jessica Ann had wanted to go, had insisted on going, even though it was only a sort of excuse. Anything to make this terrible day more ordinary.

And, too, she had felt a yearning to be inside the church. She believed in God; that was something her mother had given her—prayers and Sunday school and church had been a big part of her little life.

So when the child and her uncle and aunt pulled up outside the angular contemporary structure with its soothing sandy brick and its big circular stained glass window held together by a metallic modernistic cross, she felt a surge of hope. Birds were singing in trees whose shimmering leaves were so green they'd have been at home in Oz. Beds of tulips, their pastel bells leaning gently in the breeze, hugged the church walls.

God will not let this happen to Mommy, the child thought with a sudden certainty. He could never let such a terrible thing happen.

12

It did not occur to her, in that solitary hopeful moment, surrounded as it was by minutes and hours of dread, that God had allowed the many terrible things to occur that had led to her mother being held in a death row cell at the state prison. Gifted though the child was, she had not waded through the philosophical and theological morass of God's will as it relates to man's free will; but then, who has?

Soon, like the birds in those blindingly green, sun-reflecting trees outside, Jessica Ann was inside singing. The kids were aligned on the altar steps, the sun filtering its golden way through the looming round window's petal-like panes, as the choir director—a barrel-chested older gentleman with a kind manner and a booming voice—ran them through their two special Mother's Day numbers.

Jessica Ann's golden hair was neatly ribboned back, but still brushed her shoulders, her pale green spring frock with its floral pattern and white Peter Pan collar setting her off from the more casually dressed members of the First Baptist junior choir (Saturday morning rehearsal wasn't *real* church); of course, Jessica Ann wasn't dressed up for the rehearsal, but for what would come after. The delicately pretty, cherub-cheeked child was doing her best to get lost in the song, and it wasn't easy.

The kids were practicing "Amazing Grace," and the part about a wretch getting saved made her think of her mother. Also, the choir would be singing this on Mother's Day, and—her hopeful thoughts long since withered, any heavenly signs or insights dashed by just another typical choir practice—that made her think of how her mother would be dead by Mother's Day.

Aunt Beth and Uncle Paul were waiting at the back of the church. Other parents, scattered around the large, starkly beautiful sanctuary, watching the rehearsal, were seated in pews, but her uncle and aunt were keeping to themselves, standing behind the back row, perhaps not wanting to deal with any embarrassing questions. All over the state, the newspapers and TV had been full of what would happen today, and in small-town Ferndale this was a big event indeed. Bigger than the sesquicentennial; bigger than the flood of '93.

Jessica Ann had been living with Aunt Beth since Mommy was arrested on the murder charge; and with Uncle Paul, too, since he and Aunt Beth had gotten married just after Christmas. She had not talked to her mother since that nightmarish night in the junkyard, where the child had fled believing her mother intended to kill her. And she had not seen her mother since the day the child testified in the trial.

In the courtroom—a severe wooden chamber not unlike this one—Mommy had been sitting next to Mr. Ekhardt, her attorney, at a table, and Mommy had looked very small, almost like a child herself—wearing a simple gray suit, her hair back in a modest bun, no makeup, hands folded, like a nun. Mommy had cried as Jessica Ann testified, and so had Jessica Ann; but Jessica Ann could only know for certain that her own tears were true.

According to Aunt Beth, Jessica Ann's mother had not wanted the child to visit her at the state prison. Jessica Ann wasn't sure her aunt was telling the truth about whose idea it was that the girl not see her mother.

Her aunt and uncle were whispering to each other now, back at the rear of the sanctuary. Jessica Ann couldn't hear them, but if she could have, she would not have been surprised by the subject matter, or by their respective attitudes.

"I think this is a mistake," Beth was saying. She was a willowy brunette with large luminous brown eyes, high cheekbones, and only a hint of makeup. Her attire—a pale yellow suit with wide, faded gray stripes—was as somber as her expression.

"Not letting Jessy see her mother," Paul Conway said, "*that* would be the mistake."

He was a boyishly handsome forty, his dark hair styled slickly back; he wore a respectfully conservative brown suit, and he—like Beth—still wore the dark tan acquired on a recent Caribbean cruise.

"She's a monster," Beth said tightly. "Why put Jessica Ann through a nightmare like that?"

Conway was shocked by his wife's vehemence. He knew well how bitter Beth had become, how spiteful the events of the past year had made her.

But he also knew his wife had as good a heart as any woman he'd ever known.

"This is Jessica Ann's mother we're talking about," he said, trying to be gentle, but his disapproval coming through. "And your *sister*. . . ."

Indignation made her eyes and nostrils flare in the hardened mask of her face. "She tried to *kill* that little girl."

They kept their voices hushed, despite the intensity of their words. The last thing either of them wanted was to be overheard by any of the good churchgoing citizens of Ferndale.

"But she *didn't*," he reminded her.

"If Lieutenant March hadn't arrived . . ."

"She's always said she wouldn't have done it."

"And you believe her? My sister? A pathological liar? A sociopath?"

Beth was virtually quoting his own words back to him.

"She's a sick woman," he admitted.

"She's taking the cure today, isn't she?"

"That sounds more like your sister than you."

She glared at him. "You don't have to insult me."

He sighed as he patted the air. "You have every right to feel the way you do."

"Thank you."

"I'm just saying, if I had *my* way, they wouldn't be doing this."

Beth's mouth twitched, then settled back into an expressionless line. "It's what they do to rabid dogs."

He took her by the arms and with tender force swung her to him, though she turned her face away. "Your sister dies this afternoon. She wants to say good-bye to you . . . and to her daughter."

Beth said nothing.

"Jesus, Beth—would you deny her that?"

"Yes."

He swallowed. Nodded. "Fine. But do you want to deny it to Jessica Ann? That kid's facing the most traumatic event of her life . . . and with what she's been through, that's saying something. We have to help Jessica Ann deal with today, so that her tomorrows aren't completely screwed up—and refusing her mother's last wish, and ignoring that child's desire to see her mom one last time, is no way to start."

The words were getting to her, he could tell; but still she looked away. He had to get through to her. He had to.

"Look at me," he demanded gently. "The woman I married wasn't cruel. . . . The woman I married was a sucker for a sad movie. The woman I married cried at card tricks."

A tiny smile flickered on her lips.

"Beth . . . Think about where you are."

And Beth's eyes turned to the lovely sanctuary before them, the round stained glass window bathing golden light on the pews, the simple cross on the altar peeking between the angelic faces of singing children, children singing of redemption ("I once was lost . . ."), Jessica Ann's pretty features, so like her mother's, among them.

She folded herself into his arms. "You're right." And now the hard mask melted and he looked into pure love, and the pure loveliness of his radiant wife, and now she kidded him, saying, "You're always right."

He chuckled and gave her a peck of a kiss, which was beginning to turn into something more serious, when he drew away a bit, chiding, "Think about where you are. . . ."

She laughed a little and so did he, hugging her, comforting her, and they gazed toward the singing children and the sad sweet face of their niece.

He knew that Beth, too, needed to deal with today, whether she had any sense of that or not. Like Jessica Ann, Beth had been through so much, and had been deeply and thoroughly traumatized. Not wanting to give himself too much credit, Conway knew that he had played a big role in helping Beth hold on to her sanity.

They had met during the trial. Conway, originally a New Yorker, lately an L.A. resident, had come to cover the sensational "Killer Mommy" trial (as the supermarket tabloids had dubbed it). He'd been reluctant at first, but his editor had initially suggested, then insisted, that he make this the follow-up to his O. J. book, which had gotten lost in the shuffle of so many such volumes.

"You're ready for a comeback, kid," Ballard, his editor, had said. "You haven't hit the *Times* list since *Choked*, and that was five years ago. Your contract killer book was a stiff in hard-cover—if it wasn't for paperback, you'd be out rustling up magazine assignments and lucky to find anything."

Conway knew Ballard was right—the "Mommy" case was Midwestern through and through, and hadn't it been his heartland serial killer book—*Choked: The Mississippi Valley Strangler*—that had put him on the map as "the king of true crime"? For a while there it looked like he was going to give Ann Rule and Jack Olsen a run for their money; but when Hollywood's plans to cast Brad Pitt as the strangler fell through and sent the movie back into develop-ment hell, he was sorely in need of a new hot case.

And *The Mommy Murders* had indeed put him back on the best-seller list, with the film rights sold to Fox and Glenn Close signed to play Mrs. Sterling, "the killer mommy." If the theatrical version fell through, Cybill Shepherd was warm-ing up in the bull pen to play Mommy in a TV movie.

Meeting Beth, getting close to her in his efforts to understand this bizarre and complex case, had been a bonus Conway could never have foreseen. She was as sweet and intelligent a woman as he had ever encountered; and she was so different from the women he'd known on either coast.

Maybe it was her Midwestern upbringing;

maybe it was her domination by her beautiful older sister.

But Beth did not make the demands so many "new women" made; she was content to be his support system, to keep his house and, someday, someday soon he hoped, raise his children. He knew, from watching how good she was with Jessica Ann, that she would make a wonderful mother.

If wanting an old-fashioned girl like Beth made him shallow, so be it; if moving to a small town where he could keep a low profile and concentrate on his work made him a coward, who cared? What he'd spent on the beautiful, spacious house in Mark Twain Manor—his neighbors in the trendy development were mostly CEOs and other high-ranking executives—wouldn't have gotten him a shack in Beverly Hills, or covered a year's rent on an East Side apartment.

Up at the front of the sanctuary, the choir director released his young charges with some words of encouragement, and news of refreshments waiting downstairs, and the angels fled from the altar steps, turning instantly into unruly little devils.

"Hey hey hey!" the choir director called gruffly, peering over his half-glasses, looped around his neck on a chain. He was a grizzly in a sweater vest. "Slow down! You wanna kill somebody?"

The thundering herd had left Jessica Ann behind. This time spent inside the church not giving her what she'd wanted, what she'd so desperately needed, she trudged down the aisle, head low, spirits likewise. Her aunt met her halfway, slipping an arm around the child, while her uncle remained poised at the rear of the sanctuary.

"If you want to stay," Beth said, "for the cookies and Kool-Aid, we have time. . . ."

"I'm not hungry."

They shuffled along as the parents who'd been watching the rehearsal filed out to join their kids for refreshments downstairs.

Jessica Ann raised her head, her eyes landing momentarily on her aunt's hovering face. "I don't . . . I don't have to watch them kill her, do I?"

"No!" Beth's horrified response echoed in the chamber. A few faces turned toward her, and Beth gathered the child closer as they walked, whispering, "Of course not. . . ."

"I want to see her," Jessica Ann said, extricating herself from her aunt's loving grasp. "I want to see her, but I won't watch her die. No one can make me do that."

Paul had heard this last exchange, and he placed a hand gently on the child's shoulder.

"No one's going to," he said.

"What if Mommy wants me to?"

Beth, leaning down, said, "She won't."

Jessica Ann wasn't sure. Her mother could be pretty weird sometimes.

"You don't even have to go today," Paul said. "If you're not up for this . . ."

"I'm just not up for seeing her . . . you know . . . suffer."

Paul held the child's hand as the three of them walked out of the church into the parking lot, where the sun was shining happily, apparently unaware of what was happening below. But the birds had stopped singing, Jessica Ann noticed.

"It won't hurt," Conway said, opening the rear door of the BMW for the child. "It's just like getting a shot."

Jessica Ann smirked at this typical adult stupidity. "Are you kidding? Nothing hurts worse than a shot."

And she crawled in back, not seeing the helpless exchange of expressions between her aunt and uncle before they too got into the car and drove away, the church watching them go in mute indifference, as if it were nothing more than a building.

Chapter Two

Situated on a bluff, behind high fences topped with curls of barbed wire, overseen by a mere handful of guard towers, the modern rust-brick buildings might have been a school complex, or a government administrative center, or even a series of warehouses. The latter was most nearly right: Human beings were housed here. Only tiny, tall, narrow, barred windows indicated these structures were anything less than benign.

In fact, Oakdale Security Center, nestled in its bucolic setting, might seem an unlikely place for the state prison system's death row, but since the relatively recent reinstatement of the death penalty, and the selection of lethal injection as the method of execution, the prison hospital attached to the minimum security facility made Oakdale the logical choice.

Walking down a cement-block corridor deep within the interlocking complex of buildings, footsteps echoing like distant gunshots, Dr. John Price and attorney Neal Ekhardt were discussing Jessica Ann's mother, Mrs. Sterling.

"I want you to know," Ekhardt was saying, "how much I appreciate your efforts on my client's behalf."

The broad-shouldered attorney was a craggy, distinguished sixty-five, his snow-white hair cut military short, his all-knowing eyes peering from pouches in a face as rumpled as his somber undertaker-black suit was not, the suit's somberness slightly offset by his striped shirt and red and black patterned tie.

"She's my patient, Counselor," Price said. "And this will be the first time I've ever lost one."

"I know the feeling."

Ekhardt was the best known criminal defense attorney in the state, and this case was one of the few he had ever lost in a career that had begun in 1955.

The psychiatrist, in his round-lensed wireframes and gray sports jacket with patched elbows, might have been a professor in a small college. He was a handsome man, with dark gentle eyes, though a certain softness about his regular features betrayed his age—forty-three—and seemed at odds with the strength of his voice and his decisive mannerisms.

Price was in private practice, but also worked for the state. Two afternoons a week he spent here at Oakdale, providing prisoners with psychiatric care, as well as helping determine the sanity of certain guests of the state. He had made it clear, accepting the position, that he would not become a "professional witness" for the prosecution; he had no desire to try to shoot down insanity defenses. He had made it clear he was interested only in the welfare of his patients. Despite this, he'd gotten the job.

"You've done everything you could have, Doctor," Ekhardt said as they moved briskly down the endless corridor, "and so have I."

"It's a goddamn shame," Price said, clenching and unclenching his fists. "With this new antipsychotic drug, Mrs. Sterling could lead a normal, productive life. . . ."

But they both knew it was a case of too little, too late. They were up against a reactionary governor, about to step down, who would not likely wish to be remembered as the man who had reprieved the notorious "Killer Mommy," as the tabloid media had dubbed her.

This was the governor's last term—by law—and everyone knew who his successor would be: a very popular, and very liberal, United States senator who was coming home from Washington, D.C., to a shoo-in gubernatorial campaign.

In a matter of months, Price and Ekhardt would have been pleading Mrs. Sterling's case to a new, more sympathetic administration.

In fact, Price had already spoken to the senator's people. Not only was the state's inevitable next governor a hard-core anti–capital punishment activist, he was the kind of farsighted individual who might allow the sort of experimental program that could prove the new drug's worthiness. His advisors would no doubt counsel caution, but the next governor just might relish the political windfall of introducing the first major pharmaceutical breakthrough in criminal rehabilitation.

Bitterness and frustration edged Price's voice. "Most residents of death row linger for years before they finally . . ."

Ekhardt's laugh was a deep, humorless rumble. "You think I haven't tried? I've exhausted every possible appeal."

"I know. I know what you've been up against politically, and with the media lined up against you."

"It was a rush to judgment, all right, and it was disgraceful as hell . . . but legal."

Down the way was a window with a guard where they would check in before entering the only maximum security area in this minimum security prison.

Price grimaced, shook his head. "If we could only buy a little time. . . ."

"Time runs out for her"—and Ekhardt checked his watch—"in about one hour."

They presented their credentials (a formality, as they'd already done so on entering the facility

26

and been presented with their yellow guest badges), signed in, and were buzzed through by a morose, burly guard squatting in his underlit work area like a hound guarding the gates of hell.

Price opened the door for Ekhardt as they moved into the next corridor. It seemed colder here, and darker—the fluorescent lighting above was flickering, shorting in and out, like a bug zapper frying insects.

"I've never seen her like this," Ekhardt said, shaking his big head. "Docile . . . morose. Is there a psychiatric term for her condition?"

"Sure," Price said. "Depression. Her sister hasn't let her see her little girl in months. That child means everything to Mrs. Sterling."

Ekhardt snorted a laugh. "Can you blame the sister?" He shook a finger at the psychiatrist, almost scoldingly. "That kid's mother killed a man, right in front of her. . . ."

Price's smile was wry. "Is that how you tried to turn the governor around?"

A smirk found its way into the rumpled landscape of Ekhardt's face. "Let's face it . . . without Jessica Ann's testimony, Mommy woulda walked. They didn't even charge her with the other murders . . . if they *were* murders. . . ."

The tabloids, both print and broadcast, had convicted her of the deaths of her first two husbands; she was a classic "black widow," if you were to believe the press, though the official causes of death for Jessica Ann's father and her mother's second husband, Phillip Sterling, were drowning and heart attack, respectively.

But "the Mommy Murders" (as writer Paul Conway had anointed them in his best-selling book) had to do directly with young Jessica Ann, Mrs. Sterling's bright, painfully sheltered daughter.

Thelma Withers, the teacher who'd denied the child an outstanding student award, had apparently fallen to her death from a ladder right before Mrs. Sterling showed up for a parent-teacher conference. The coveted plaque, known to be in the teacher's room at the time, was missing, and never recovered. The coroner's report deemed the teacher's broken neck inconsistent with the supposed fall, and foul play was suspected.

Leann Jones, the McKinley School janitor rumored to have heard Mrs. Sterling and Mrs. Withers talking (contradicting Mrs. Sterling's claim that the teacher was already dead when she arrived for the conference), had been electrocuted in the grade school's furnace room in a bizarre accident that had the janitor falling against a breaker board while standing in a pool of water from her own spilled bucket. There were those who believed Leann Jones died when some unknown party splashed her with water while she was standing at the breaker board . . . and that unknown person was thought to be Mrs. Sterling.

Then there was Mark Patterson, who had gone undercover (and under Mrs. Sterling's covers) investigating the death of Phillip Sterling for Consolidated Life. Patterson had been talking to Jessica Ann in the middle of the night, when Mrs. Sterling entered and shot him, claiming Patterson had gotten sexually abusive with her earlier in the evening and that she was fearful he might be molesting Jessica Ann.

But at the trial, Jessica Ann had admitted that her mother had told her not to tell anyone that her mommy had, prior to killing him before her daughter's shocked eyes, discovered that her new boyfriend was an insurance investigator.

Patterson's was the only murder the woman had been charged with, but its cold-blooded nature had been enough to put her here, in this bland cement-block hospital corridor that was the state's death row. And who among the jurors could honestly say that their media-driven knowledge of the other "murders" hadn't hung over their judgment?

"Do you think she killed them?" Price asked the attorney. His patient had never admitted to any wrongdoing, but he had pretty much convinced himself that she was guilty and that this insistence on innocence was a part of her pathology—though he still had doubts that this lovely woman could be the homicidal psychopath of the tabloids.

Ekhardt paused and smiled half a smile, eyes twinkling like a leprechaun's. "Don't ask me to break confidentiality with my client," he said, "and I won't ask you to betray patient-doctor privilege."

Price sighed and stopped the attorney with a gentle hand on the elbow; the two men faced each other, eyes locked. "Ekhardt—if she's the monster everyone says she is, why do we both care about what happens to her?"

"Because," the attorney said with the most world-weary smile Price had ever seen, "she's the damnedest case either one of us has ever had."

At the end of the corridor, on the left, under the flickery, buzzing fluorescent lighting, waited the doorway to the lethal injection chamber. On either side of the door, leaning against the wall like cigar store Indians, were Lieutenant March and his partner, Sergeant Anderson.

In a respectfully dark tie, and a pale blue shirt cut by his shoulder holster, March—whose dogged, Columbo-like tracking of Mrs. Sterling had resulted in the woman's arrest—was a sturdy looking sixty years of age, gray touching only the sideburns of his brown hair, possessed of a bored, basset-hound expression and surprisingly kind eyes under wild tangles of eyebrow. He was Ferndale's chief of detectives, and a former Chicago homicide cop; he had come to the little town looking for a low-key work environment and had found instead Mrs. Sterling.

Price was better acquainted with Anderson, a local boy who had attached himself to March, to pick up on the older cop's big-city savvy. March could be something of a slob (though not in this instance), while Anderson had a reputation for vanity and often looked dapper.

Today was no exception: Longish brown hair gelled back, ruggedly handsome with narrow eyes and a hawk nose, Anderson slouched against the wall, chewing gum, conveying contempt and arrogance, but looking swell in his light brown sports coat with a dark tie and his trademark suspenders. His holstered gun was clipped inside his waistband.

Noting the glum expressions of the approaching attorney and psychiatrist, March brightened. "Well . . . looks like the governor didn't name Mrs. Sterling Mother of the Year."

"Nobody likes a sore winner, March," Ekhardt said, rolling up like a tank and stopping before the detective. He regarded March with eyes that were slits of contempt. "You really relish seeing a woman die?"

"This one I do," March said, nodding, and it was clear he was telling the truth, though the smugness was gone.

"Is she in the chamber?" Ekhardt asked, with a nod toward the door between the two cops.

"No," Anderson said, chewing gum, quietly insolent. "She's in visitation—saying good-bye to her little girl. . . . A touching moment between a mother and the child she tried to strangle."

It was March and Anderson who had caught up with Mrs. Sterling and Jessica Ann, after mother and child had taken flight. It had ended in a junkyard, where the child had fled from a motel room, hiding from the mother she had come to believe was going to kill her.

"Drop by my office, Anderson," Price said with quiet contempt. He turned his scornful gaze on March. "You, too, Lieutenant. I'll work you guys into group therapy—no charge."

March laughed at that a little, exchanging murmurs of sarcastic gratitude with Anderson, while the psychiatrist and the attorney settled against the wall opposite the two cops, opposing forces digging in, facing the door behind which the patient of one and the client of the other would die.

Chapter Three

Her mother was already seated at the head of the picnic-style table in the bleak, cement-block room when Jessica Ann got there. The room had another such table on either side of this one, and was large enough to accommodate a good number of prisoners and their families on visiting day.

But only one family would gather in this space today.

The child, in the backseat of the BMW, had watched as Oakdale prison rose from the green, peaceful Iowa countryside like a brick apparition, her eyes wide with barbed wire and guard towers. They stopped at a guard booth, with Uncle Paul sitting behind the steering wheel as if he were ordering takeout food but instead presenting papers and identification. A chain-link gate was opened for them, yawning open automatically. They drove around behind the large blocky buildings into a parking lot that was almost empty. In fact, the BMW was the only car in the row of visitor spaces.

Soon they were in an area where the cement-block walls were washed pale, pale yellow. The uniformed woman at the window just inside the building—after Uncle Paul signed a lot of papers and received their three yellow visitor's badges—had sent them to wait here, near double doors, one of which was marked VISITATION, the other NO SMOKING; the woman had referred to this as the reception area, but there were no chairs or anything. Even the health clinic gave you a chair and some old magazines to look at. It was as though, Jessica Ann thought, they didn't want you to stay long.

That was okay with her.

The guard standing watch outside the two doors was like a bear in a person suit, a towering figure with sad eyes and a neatly trimmed beard, wearing a white shirt with elaborate official patches on either sleeve and dark pants with a white stripe down either pant leg. The guard stared straight ahead, not acknowledging the presence of Jessica Ann and her aunt and uncle. Jessica Ann couldn't tell whether he was keeping people from going in or going out.

Uncle Paul gave their names to the big, sad-eyed guard, who only nodded, not writing them down on a clipboard or anything; apparently they were expected. The guard opened the door for them—the child looked right up at him, to see if he was avoiding their gaze; he was—and Uncle Paul stepped inside, with Aunt Beth, whose arm was around Jessica Ann's shoulders, guiding the child into the large room, which was as cold as it looked.

Mommy looked so small, seated down at the head of that table. The perfect arcs of her icy blond hair framed the lovely face as always, but the finely chiseled features were untouched by makeup, which wasn't like Mommy. The petite woman's slender, shapely frame was indiscernible within the bright orange pajama-like prison garb. Her mother had lost weight, Jessica Ann noted; and she had never seen her mother look so pale.

As they entered, Beth guiding Jessica Ann down the aisle between tables, toward Mommy, the prisoner sat with her hands folded prayerfully before her and watched them with hooded eyes, the mask of her face broken only by a tiny smile, a comforting sort of smile that Jessica Ann knew was intended only for her.

Behind Mommy stood a female guard, a pretty woman with dark reddish blond hair cut in a style similar to Mommy's; she was as small as the guard outside was big, and seemed almost as lost in her white blouse with its fancy insignia shoulder patches and men's dark white-striped pants as Mommy did in the prisoner's uniform. The pretty guard stood rigidly erect, staring into nothing, her expression as empty as a baby's.

Beth guided Jessica Ann to a chair near her mother; the places where the child's skin touched the metal folding chair seemed ice-cube cold. Then the child's aunt took a chair herself, just behind the girl, at the adjacent table, while Paul positioned himself on the periphery, as if he— like the guard—were merely keeping watch, not wanting to intrude on this painfully private family moment. Jessica Ann understood that. Paul was family now, but he hadn't been when the bad things happened.

For a while Mommy sat somewhat slumped— an unusual posture for her—with her head bowed, which with her folded hands further suggested prayer, but Jessica Ann didn't think her mother was praying. The eyes, hooded though they were, were staring, staring into private thoughts. Perhaps her mother was trying to gather the proper words to say good-bye; or perhaps her mother was mentally rehearsing a speech that she had prepared in her cell on death row.

Finally Mommy began to speak, but still she did not look at Jessica Ann.

"I know there's nothing I can say to make it up to either of you," Mommy said.

Jessica Ann swallowed; the sound of her mother's voice, so musical, so rich, so deep, so comforting, sent a shiver up the child's spine.

"But I've had a lot of time to think," Mommy

said. She twitched a tight smile. "And when I look back on my life, I see two people that mean a lot to me. . . ."

And now Mommy lifted her chin, swiveled her head, and looked past Jessica Ann, at the child's aunt.

"Beth, you were always there," Mommy said. It was part benediction, part admission. Then, almost as an afterthought, she granted her sister's reward for a lifetime of service: "Thank you."

Jessica Ann peeked back at Aunt Beth, who swallowed, nodded. The child was almost surprised to see the tears welling in her aunt's eyes, knowing how bitter Beth had become about Mommy. But Jessica Ann understood; much as Beth may have tried to steel herself for this moment, the emotions in her would brim nonetheless.

Funny. The gray stripes on Beth's pale yellow suit made her look like the prisoner.

"Jessica Ann," Mommy said.

Swallowing, gripped by fear and affection, the child swung her gaze away from her aunt and back to her mother.

With an uncharacteristic gentleness, even sweetness, and with her pale blue eyes locked upon the identical eyes of her daughter, the mother said, "I know I scared you."

Jessica Ann lowered her gaze.

The mother leaned toward her child but did not reach out to her, the lovely tapering fingers of either hand still intertwined prayerfully. She spoke as if she were speaking to a younger child than Jessica Ann.

But then Jessica Ann had been younger when they'd last spoken. In that junkyard.

And it was of that meeting that her mother now spoke.

"I know you think I was going to hurt you."

Jessica Ann lifted her eyes to her mother's, tentatively. "You didn't hurt me . . ." But one hand reflexively rose to the neck her mother's hands had gripped on that terrible night. ". . . much."

"When I saw your face in the moonlight," the woman said, almost dreamily, as if recalling a wonderful shared moment between mother and daughter, ". . . I couldn't hurt you. I could never hurt you." And she smiled and lifted her shoulders in a sort of shrug. "You're a part of *me*."

Jessica Ann nodded. "I know, Mommy."

Mommy leaned closer and the prayerful hands came apart and those two graceful, powerful hands took one of the child's in them, gently, lovingly. But some of the tenderness was out of Mommy's voice, replaced by an insistence as the woman said, "And I'm a part of *you*."

Swallowing back the tears, Jessica Ann nodded. "I know, Mommy. I know. . . ."

"And I still will be, even if I'm gone."

Nodding, the child gave her mother a smile of comfort, of assurance. "I know . . . I know. . . ."

The female guard, who had not seemed to be paying any attention to them, suddenly leaned down between them, like the blade of a tollgate falling; there was surprising reluctance in her action, and equally surprising compassion in her voice as she said, "It's time. . . . I'm sorry."

Mommy's smile was like a child's as she squeezed Jessica Ann's hand, laughing gently as she asked her daughter, "Who's your best friend?"

It was the old ritual, dating beyond the beginning of the child's memory, a ritual Jessica Ann had dreaded and yet come to depend on, because it was the one way her mother had ever found to say, *I love you*.

"You are, Mommy."

There was a musical lilt to Mommy's voice; it sounded so beautiful to Jessica Ann, and so sad.

"Who loves you," Mommy asked, "more than anything on God's green earth?"

Jessica Ann nodded and nodded. "You do, Mommy."

"That's right," Mommy laughed softly, "that's right. . . ."

Somehow it was a moment of triumph between mother and daughter—triumph over the adversity they had survived together, triumph over the terrible thing Mommy had almost done to her, triumph over the death that would soon separate them. Nothing could come between Jessica Ann and her mother.

But a sudden old coldness came back into Mommy's voice as she said, almost scolding, definitely warning her daughter, "Don't *ever* forget it."

Taken aback, Jessica Ann gulped and nodded and said, in the tone of a six-year-old, "No, Mommy."

And then Paul stepped in closer, to pull the chair out for Jessica Ann, and Beth was at the girl's side, gently pulling her to her feet, and Jessica Ann and her mother held on to each other's hands until the child's aunt tugged her away. Jessica Ann could barely hold back the tears, and she was shaking her head, saying, "No, no, no," or was she just thinking it?

But as she drew away from her mother, she could not remember ever having seen so much love in her mother's face, except perhaps for that moment in the junkyard, in the moonlight, when Mommy had decided not to kill her.

And as Beth gathered Jessica Ann up, ushering her from the room, Paul Conway was nudging the metal chair back in place against the table, about to go with his wife and niece, when Mrs. Sterling called to him.

"Paul . . . please . . . a moment, please. . . ."

This was all Jessica Ann heard, as her aunt escorted her into the chairless reception area. The child was not privy to the brief conversation that followed between her uncle and her mother.

"Yes?" Conway asked, startled that the girl's mother had even acknowledged his presence, let alone singled him out for attention.

Mrs. Sterling gestured, a tentative, weak gesture unlike her. "Paul . . . Paul, I know I haven't been very warm to you."

He ambled closer, rested his fingertips on the back of the metal chair. A small, wry smile formed. "Why should you be? I make a fortune out of writing your story, and then steal your sister from you."

Her gaze was an appraising one, like a scientist studying a germ under a microscope. "This was your doing, today, wasn't it? Talking Beth into letting me say good-bye. . . ."

He swallowed, nodded his admission.

She twitched a smile. "Thank you for that, anyway."

They had been adversaries of sorts; through her attorney, Ekhardt, she had threatened to sue him over his book, which had been yet another bone of contention between Beth and her sister— as if almost killing Jessica Ann hadn't wedged enough of a wall between them.

"Hell," Paul said with a chuckle, "it'll make a good scene if I ever write a sequel."

Mrs. Sterling huffed a humorless laugh, glancing around the death chamber, raising an eyebrow.

"Looks like a short sequel," she said.

The remark froze him momentarily, then with no further words between them, Conway withdrew to the reception area, handing his yellow visitor's badge to the burly bearded guard.

Lieutenant March was waiting, keeping a respectful distance. He had come to help escort his prisoner to her death. He was down by a trash receptacle, taking a draw off the cigarette he'd just confiscated from the guard who'd been ignoring the NO SMOKING sign; March sucked one last drag from it, then deposited the cigarette in the receptacle and leaned back against the cement wall, waiting, pretending not to eavesdrop.

Conway joined Beth, whose arm held Jessica Ann close to her side.

"What did she say to you?" Beth wondered.

"Good-bye," he said.

Jessica Ann was looking toward the closed door to the visitation room. "Are they going to kill her in there?"

A hand flew to Beth's face in horror.

Conway, quietly, matter-of-factly, said, "No, honey. . . ."

He knelt to face the child. Beth was looking on, admiring the rapport he'd developed with her niece.

Trying to put gentleness in the harsh words, he said, "They'll take her to a room called the Lethal Injection Chamber. . . ."

Beth winced.

Writer or not, he was searching for the right language as the child's sky-blue eyes regarded him with what seemed like bland indifference. "Different states do it different ways. . . . Do you know what a drip is?"

"Yeah," Jessica Ann said, and she nodded back toward Lieutenant March. "Him."

His pretense of not listening crumbled as

March smiled a little, as if he couldn't blame the child for her opinion. Then he again stared straight ahead.

Conway smiled briefly, then said, "You may have a point, but, well . . . in some states, they put an IV in the person's arm, and in that hanging plastic bag, they add, well . . ."

"Poison," the child finished. "What do they do in this state?"

Her matter-of-factness was throwing him. But Conway pressed on: "Just like you said, she gets a shot. And you're right, I'm sure it does hurt, like any shot hurts . . . but just a little. And then she goes to sleep."

"And never wakes up."

Conway exchanged a tragic glance with his wife. "Yes."

Suddenly Jessica Ann hugged Conway, startling him, clutching him desperately. "I know she did bad things, I know she did bad things, but I don't want her to die. . . ."

Conway looked helplessly toward Beth, whose hand was covering her mouth, tears welling. He said, "I know you don't, honey."

"I prayed," the child blurted, hugging him, hugging him tight. "I prayed they wouldn't kill her. I prayed and prayed. Do you think God heard?"

Leaning in, Beth eased a hand onto her niece's shoulder. "I'm *sure* He heard."

Jessica Ann looked up and back at her aunt, the child's eyes swimming with tears and terror and despair. "But . . . did He *listen*?"

Chapter Four

Jessica Ann and her aunt and uncle were on their way back to Ferndale by the time the child's mother, strapped onto a hospital gurney, was rolled down the hall by the somber, bearded, burly guard.

There was no point in the little family being present in the prison when Jessica Ann's mother was executed; state law required an autopsy, and the body would not even be released to the family's mortician until the middle of next week. No funeral had been scheduled, only a small graveside service was planned.

These wishes were among the rare instances where Beth and the woman strapped onto the gurney had found issues to agree upon.

Certainly Mrs. Sterling already looked like a

corpse, albeit an exquisite one, her face inanimate, eyes wide and clear and empty and blue, black security straps cutting across the Day-Glo orange of her prison uniform, as the journey down the long hallway continued, the buzzing fluorescent lighting gleaming off the chrome of the black-cushioned cart. Trailing behind the bearded guard, on either side of him, and slowly marching in solemn procession, came Lieutenant March and police guard Carol Totter, the attractive copper-haired unmarried woman of thirty-five who had witnessed the final meeting between mother and daughter in the visitation area.

Sergeant Anderson held open the door as the guard wheeled the prisoner into the Lethal Injection Chamber, an anonymous white-walled cement-block room with a single narrow, barred window, barely more than a cubicle and empty but for a shining metal tray table. Lieutenant March resumed his position outside the room by the door opposite the waiting Dr. Price and attorney Ekhardt; but Guard Carol Totter followed the gurney inside and assumed a "parade rest" position near the far wall.

Soon, the prisoner's attorney and psychiatrist had been admitted into the chamber for final conferences with their client/patient, with only the female guard keeping them company within the room. Once the door was shut behind them, the chamber was sealed off; soundproofed, the room was meat-locker chilly, an air conditioner

46

harshly whispering its rebuke from a single over-head, overworked vent.

"Neal," Mrs. Sterling said softly.

Like a knight answering his lady's summons, the broad-shouldered attorney went to her side as she lay immobilized by the trio of wide black straps crossing her torso. He leaned near her, his weathered, lined face settling into a gentle smile that showed only support, not pity. His relationship with this woman went back many years, and had not always been strictly client-attorney in nature.

"Is there anything I can do for you?" he asked, his gravelly voice touched with tenderness.

With her eyes she called him nearer.

She whispered, "The envelope I left with you?"

"Yes . . ."

"It's a list of safe deposit boxes. Put everything into a trust fund for Jessica Ann."

"Done," he nodded.

The martyr on the gurney bestowed upon him a smile of dismissal, and he withdrew from her side, puzzled—like so many men before him—as to why and how this cold creature could elicit such feelings of warmth within him.

Dr. Price took Ekhardt's place at her side. "In this state," Price said, "you have a right to have your personal physician present, during the, uh . . . Do you want me to . . . ?"

She shook her head, wincing. Her expression was one of compassion for her doctor. "No, John, I don't want you to see this. Thank you. . . ." She turned her head, to take in Ekhardt as well. "Thank you both for what you've . . . attempted to do for me."

The psychiatrist and attorney exchanged brief expressions of disappointment; she had expressed her gratitude but not quite granted them forgiveness for failing her.

When the attorney and psychiatrist exited, they resumed their positions against the wall, opposite the two plainclothes cops who stood on either side of the chamber door.

Within minutes, Dr. Thomas Black, in a suit and tie that reflected his last name, entered through the doorway down at the end of the long narrow hall; carried before him, in fig-leaf fashion, was his black bag. On his heels were Warden Munsey and his personal escort, a heavyset uniformed officer with a mustache and a jutting jaw. The warden had steel-gray hair, dark-rimmed glasses, and a neatly trimmed thatch of white beard that gave his long face the dour countenance of abolitionist John Brown. Throwing long, ominous shadows, they moved slowly forward in somber lockstep, as if in a funeral, rather than on their way to create one.

Sergeant Anderson opened the door to the chamber for them and they seemed to glide in like ghosts. March joined the procession as Anderson shut them all inside.

Quickly, March moved to the prisoner's side. His mouth twitched in something that was neither smile nor frown, and he said, "I understand you declined the chaplain."

She gazed up at him in cool contempt. "I'm at peace with myself."

March nearly laughed; that this multiple murderer could marshal such indignation and self-pity was yet another of Mrs. Sterling's long list of amazing accomplishments.

But instead—feeling a grudging respect for his adversary, and a closeness that is known by pursuer and pursued—he said only, "Hey . . . that's more than I can say."

Now was not the time to gloat. Eyes fixed not uncompassionately upon the woman he had brought to this deadly room, March solemnly crossed himself.

"I'm a Baptist," she said, casually caustic. "But thanks."

He took that punishment—after all, she was about to take hers, wasn't she?—and said, "The warden has to read something official."

March faded back as the warden stepped forward, his massive uniformed escort jockeying for position behind him like the world's largest little tin soldier. Dr. Black, head lowered, the black bag clutched before him, stood by the shining metal tray-stand.

"Mrs. Sterling," the warden said, as if acknowledging her at a fund-raiser, and he withdrew the document from within his brown suitcoat. He cleared his throat rather grandiosely; in his line of work, the warden, though a politician, seldom had the opportunity to give a speech.

"In the name of the people and the governor of this state," his said, his sonorous voice ringing and pinging off the walls of the cement chamber, "we carry out sentence on this day of May seventeenth, for the capital crime of first-degree murder. . . . And may God have mercy on your soul."

The warden turned to go, but was stopped by Mrs. Sterling, who said, "And yours," with quiet, dignified contempt.

Slightly rattled, the warden—followed by his giant tin soldier—exited; March was the last one out, giving his prisoner one last long look, as if to convey his agreement with the harsh but just sentence. She was not looking his way, however; her eyes were on the cement ceiling.

Just as March shut the door, sealing her within the soundproofed chamber in the company of Dr. Black and guard Totter, Mrs. Sterling was startled by the doctor placing the black bag on the tray-stand where its metal feet made a clangy *clunk*.

Dr. Black was a small dark man whose pockmarked face was an oval emphasized by a slightly receding hairline; his features held no more expression than those of a manikin, and his dark eyes looked only at the various items he had begun to systematically remove from the black bag and place on the shining tray—surgical gloves, rubber tourniquet, hypodermic needle, and a vial of a dark fluid that was not medicine.

Dr. Black stood just behind Mrs. Sterling, near that tray, and occasionally she would look back at him, attracted first by the sound of the doctor tearing a rubber glove as he tried to snug it on. He had to retrieve a second pair from the bag. His slight fumbling putting on the replacement pair further attracted her notice, and she watched as he held the plastic-shielded hypo and vial of dark fluid in trembling hands.

The doctor approached her and, as he was tying her bare arm with the rubber tourniquet, she asked in a friendly, almost soothing manner, "If you don't mind my saying so . . . you seem a little bit nervous."

"Please," he said, and his voice cracked like an adolescent's. "This will be over quickly . . . don't make it harder on—"

"Either of us than it has to be?" She smiled, just a little; but even Mrs. Sterling's faintest smiles could be dazzling. She studied him, appraised him. "This is your first time, isn't it?"

"Please. . . ."

"Mine, too."

He tore open a packaged alcohol swab and applied it to her arm beneath the tourniquet.

"Afraid of infection?" she asked.

"Please," he said, and swallowed. He tried not to look at her. "I'd prefer we not talk."

The doctor stepped to the tray and she looked back at him, as he injected the needle into the lifted vial, filling it with death. The doctor no longer seemed nervous as he gave the hypo a ghastly test squirt, and in a moment, the needle was poised at her exposed, throbbing vein.

"Doctor!" Mrs. Sterling pulled her arm back, tried vainly to sit up, straining at her straps, her composure suddenly transformed into torment. "Doctor—a moment, please! I made a mistake . . . a terrible mistake. . . ."

And now, finally, the doctor looked at her. Like anyone who had followed the "Killer Mommy" case in the media (and that was everyone), Dr. Black knew that Mrs. Sterling had never admitted any guilt, had always clung to her innocence. Perhaps now he would hear her deathbed confession. . . .

"I refused the chaplain," she said pitifully, "and I shouldn't have. I want to pray, I *need* to pray. . . ."

Drawing the needle away from her flesh, the doctor drew a breath, and paused. Then the breath emerged, with the words, "All right. Take a few moments. . . ."

And he bowed his head, closed his eyes, and began a silent prayer of his own.

"Unstrap my wrists," she pleaded softly.

His eyes snapped open, and were on her face again; she had his eyes now and had no intention of letting them go.

"Unstrap my wrists so I can fold my hands," she explained earnestly. "So I can bow my head and pray properly."

His head reared back, as if he'd been slapped. "I can't . . . that's impossible. . . ."

"Please! Please . . ." The woman's eyes brimmed with tears. "I want to pray. I need to pray." A strained nobility entered her voice. "Don't send me into darkness without the light of God to guide me."

The doctor, however, still was not sure, looking away, saying, "I'm sorry, I just *can't*. . . ."

"Doctor."

The tone of Mrs. Sterling's voice, in that one word, had completely changed: She had issued a command.

He again looked into the haunting china-blue eyes of the patient the state was paying him to lose.

"Tonight," Mrs. Sterling said accusingly, "when you try to go to sleep, remember me, Doctor—remember the woman you murdered . . . whose pitiful last request you refused."

And her chin crinkled, her mouth trembled, in a dignified effort to hold back her tears.

Dr. Black looked plaintively across the gurney at Guard Totter, who stood facing forward, as if she had heard not a word of any of this.

But she had. Guard Totter had become very close to her prisoner over these last months. In fact, the prisoner wore a gold ankle bracelet given to her as an expression of affection by the guard.

Totter's head swung toward the doctor and her cold policewoman mask melted into heartbroken sympathy, and she nodded to him, a nod of consent, of assurance that this one last charitable act toward the condemned presented no danger.

Totter was smiling at Mrs. Sterling when the first strap was removed, and the prisoner with a swiftness like a pouncing cat reached for the black bag on the tray and swung it into the doctor's head, knocking him to the floor, and continuing that swift motion around, did the same to Totter.

Totter was unconscious before she hit the floor, bleeding next to the flung bag and its scattered contents, and did not see Mrs. Sterling, eyes gleaming like the steel tray-stand, quickly unstrap herself and move toward the fallen doctor, closing in.

In the hallway, Lieutenant March and Sergeant Anderson, standing vigil across from the door, and Ekhardt and Price, waiting solemnly just down the hallway a few steps, heard none of this; the soundproofed chamber had protected them as they waited for the long terrible moments behind that door to elapse.

March was pacing, Anderson leaning against the wall, when the door swung slowly partway open and, head lowered, Dr. Black—his face a grave, putty mask—appeared in the crack.

The deed, March thought, sighing heavily, *is done*.

Then the door flew open wide to reveal that Black was the hostage of Mrs. Sterling, who held him before her as a human shield even as she pressed the hypo's tip to the doctor's trembling neck.

March turned, bumping into Anderson, unintentionally pinning his partner there and keeping the younger cop from reacting, and reflexively drew his automatic from its shoulder harness.

But Mrs. Sterling—her smile bewitching, glamorous, crazed—merely watched him, unconcerned.

Cool-eyed, as self-composed as a country club hostess, she gazed over the shoulder of the wide-eyed, sweating doctor, whose neck was dimpling from the needle she was pressing there. As calmly as if calling upon members of the PTA to volunteer for a bake sale, she said, "I'm going to need a driver. Any volunteers?"

March was training the automatic on her. Anderson had drawn his weapon, too.

"You're not walking out of here," March said firmly. "It's not going to happen."

Raising a regal eyebrow as if to say, "Really?", Mrs. Sterling walked the doctor along the wall, even as she pressed the needle into his flesh; a teardrop of blood formed, her thumb poised over the plunger, ready to inject the doctor lethally.

"Then the boys at med school," she said, "are going to have a familiar cadaver."

The two cops, guns in hand, moved into the middle of the hallway, following her as she dragged the doctor toward the distant doorway, swiveling to keep her hostage between her and the police. Ekhardt and Price clung like flies to the wall opposite.

"Don't *do* this," the attorney said softly. Something like anguish was in his voice.

"Neal," she replied evenly, guiding the banjo-eyed Black along, "I think from here on out I'll handle my own defense. . . . Dr. Price! You up for driving?"

Price nodded unenthusiastically.

"Give it up, Mrs. Sterling!" March said. He had the automatic trained on her, at least on that small part of her that could be seen past the sweat-beaded doctor.

But, walking backward, Mrs. Sterling kept moving herself and her hostage toward the door at the far end, the needle indenting the flesh of his neck and weeping blood drops.

March issued a final warning: "Mrs. Sterling . . ."

She was smiling over the doctor's shoulder at the cop, still moving, the smile almost daring him, inviting him to shoot.

He did.

The shot rang out in the enclosed space like an ungodly thunderbolt. March had chosen his moment carefully and, much as he might have preferred to put a bullet in that pretty head, his best bet had been her shoulder, which was where it caught her, the shoulder of the hand holding the needle, a needle that now went flying as her hostage sprang loose from custody and ran pell-mell, scared shitless, past March to hell and gone, as simultaneously the impact of the shot slammed the woman into the wall, where she slid down, leaving a smudgy red trail.

Then Mrs. Sterling sat there, clutching her shoulder with the hand of her good arm, blood oozing through in scarlet trickles. Her head was held high, defiant till the last.

Price rushed to her, cradled her in his arms.

"Don't just stand there!" he called. "She needs immediate attention!"

But March wasn't standing, he was weaving; it was as if he were the one who'd been shot. He dropped to the floor, the gun tumbling from the hand of an arm that sharp pain was traveling up, practically paralyzing him.

Anderson, forced by circumstance into a bystander's role, flew to his partner's side, hovering over the older detective, saying, "Bill! Bill, are you all right?"

The gunshot had been heard; an alarm bell began a droning, electronic clanging.

March's reply was oddly thick, his speech slurred. "Nuh . . . nuh-never . . . never bet- better."

"Bill . . ."

March looked beyond his partner toward his prisoner's attorney, standing nearby. Ekhardt, flabbergasted by this turn of events, was looking from his wounded client to the fallen detective, as if memorizing facts for future use in court.

"Well, Ekhardt," March said curtly, clutching his bad arm with his good one, his speech clear again, "looks like your client found a way to buy herself a reprieve after all. . . ."

Anderson, crouched by March, impulsively reached for his partner's weapon and thrust the automatic forward, toward the fallen prisoner, whether to keep her covered or to shoot, it wasn't clear to Ekhardt, who reached out and shoved the cop's arm down.

But he didn't speak to Anderson.

"You know the law, Lieutenant," Ekhardt said to March, his smile tight and threatening.

Still, it was Anderson who replied bitterly, "Yeah—you can't execute a prisoner until or unless they're perfectly healthy . . . wouldn't be civilized."

March, breathing hard, blinking away at a sudden blinding headache, had to wonder, as the younger detective helped him to his feet, if that hadn't been the object all along.

After all, down the hall, where she was cradled in the arms of her psychiatrist, below a smear of blood tracing an abstract design on the cement-block wall, the mother of Jessica Ann Sterling was smiling.

TWO:

A Mother's Redemption

Chapter Five

The needle poised to go into Mrs. Sterling's arm was in the older, experienced hands of Dr. Clarence Stern, Oakdale Security's senior physician, who had performed two lethal injections for the state of Iowa in the year that had passed since the escape attempt. (Dr. Black no longer worked for the state; he had relocated to Kentucky and was in private practice.)

In the corridor outside the chamber—the same corridor where Mrs. Sterling had attempted her escape, where the wall had been streaked red with the prisoner's own blood—the repercussions of that escape attempt upon Oakdale prison's now stepped-up security policy were reflected in the heavily armed contingency of guards who had accompanied her here.

61

An absurd formality, considering that this death row prisoner would be released tomorrow.

"This is just a local," the doctor said as the hypo pumped its fluid into her system. Dr. Stern was tall, sallow, with an oblong face, dark hair, and dark-rimmed Coke-bottle glasses. His words were friendly enough, but his manner was lugubrious. "To make the insertion of the implant itself painless."

Mrs. Sterling, attired in an orange prison jumpsuit, was seated in a brown leather geriatric recliner in the cementblock examining room.

"Will there be a scar, Doctor?" Mrs. Sterling asked, watching the Doctor withdraw the needle.

He twitched a smile, adjusted the glasses, his eyes like a bug's behind the thick lenses.

"A tiny one," he admitted. "And a bit of a bump on your forearm, where the flexible silicon rod is tucked under the skin. . . . No cause for alarm—this is strictly an outpatient procedure, Mrs. Sterling."

"I see. How often is it replaced?"

"Only twice a year. You will have to come back to Oakdale to see me. I hope you don't find that too unpleasant a prospect."

"Of course not, Doctor," she said, bestowing a smile on him. "I'm ready. You can go ahead. I'm not by nature squeamish."

Another adjustment of the glasses. "You understand your medication will be released continuously, in a small, measured dose. . . ."

"Sort of like a time-release cold capsule?"

"Exactly."

She gazed at him beseechingly, and as he looked into the china-blue eyes in the lovely face, the doctor understood for a moment how his younger colleague could have been fooled by this woman, the year before.

"Tell me, Doctor," she asked, "will I still be me?"

But it was a question better suited for a specialist in mental health, and the next afternoon, in the office of the psychiatrist who would be both her medical overseer and, in effect, her parole officer, she got an answer.

"You're still you," Dr. John Price said.

Price was seated behind his desk in the masculine, wood-paneled office. His patient was by the large window facing the parking lot, pacing like a caged panther, her drab prison attire replaced by a businesslike yet very feminine pale pink suit.

For two years he had known only the woman in formless prison orange, and seeing the shapeliness of her, the lovely nyloned legs, the beautiful face with its perfectly, subtly applied makeup, was disconcerting, somehow.

"New and improved," she said, her bitterness understated but very much present. "Like a laundry detergent."

This was not the severe cubicle at Oakdale where they had had so many sessions during her incarceration, but Price's private office at Towncrest Medical Center on the outskirts of Ferndale. Soft classical Muzak filtered in, and pastel floral watercolors sought to soothe patients' troubled sensibilities.

Now she was behind him, plucking from atop a mahogany two-drawer file a framed photograph of his attractive, dark-haired wife, examining it with a clinical smirk.

He took the framed photo from her, as if removing something dangerous from the hands of a child, and placed the picture on his desk, saying, "Your violent behavior has a biochemical basis."

She appeared utterly bored. "So I understand."

"This antipsychotic drug short-circuits your aggressive impulses."

"I've always liked designer clothing." She picked up a small framed photo of his young son, Jason, from his desk, looked at it, returned it dismissively. "Now I'll have a designer brain." Her half-lidded, half-smiling expression was patronizing. "My wardrobe will be complete."

"You had a choice," Price said firmly, gesturing toward her arm. "Lethal injection or that implant."

She touched her sleeve. "Quite a choice. . . . This burns terribly; it's very red."

"Didn't the doctor at Oakdale give you anything for pain or inflammation?"

"No. Dr. Stern definitely did not have your bedside manner." She had her back to him, fiddling with the thin white window blinds.

"I'll give you a prescription before you go," he

said, frustrated by her put-upon attitude. "You'd better keep in mind that you're very much a trial case . . . a social experiment."

She turned to him and a faint sneer formed on the cold, lovely face. "A guinea pig?"

Price shrugged, nodded. "But a *live* one. If this doesn't work out—or if you get cute and remove that implant—the next shot you get will either be back at Oakdale . . . or from Max Anderson's automatic."

" 'Max'?" She seemed amused by the familiarity. "Is Sergeant Anderson a friend of yours?"

"We went to high school together."

"Small-town life is so . . . precious."

"He was a hardheaded SOB then, and he's a hardheaded SOB now. He doesn't just carry a grudge—he thrives on it."

She shrugged. "Is it my fault his friend March had a stroke?"

"After the stress of your attempted jailbreak? Anderson certainly thinks so."

March was off the force, retired with full disability, sitting at home with the right side of his body paralyzed. He had the best of round-the-clock care—the former Chicago detective had married well, to a wealthy widow he'd met in town, on a case—but his career, his life as an active man, seemed over.

Price had no great love for March, and perhaps his unforgiving stance on Mrs. Sterling had bought the cop this bad karma; but he pitied such an active man turning into an invalid. And

Mrs. Sterling's callousness troubled, even angered the psychiatrist.

Perhaps these thoughts showed on his face, because suddenly Mrs. Sterling's chilly expression melted into sweetness as she came around the desk, high heels clicking on the parquet floor, and climbed into Price's lap, slipping her arms around his neck.

"John . . . don't think I'm ungrateful," she said with the old intimacy. "I know what you've done for me. You've saved my life."

And she kissed him, a tiny, tender peck of gratitude.

"Not here," he said, swallowing. "Not in the office. . . ."

Then she removed his glasses, tossed them onto the desk, turned the framed photo of his wife facedown, and kissed him again, deeply, her tongue dueling his, pushing herself into him to where his chair nearly tipped over.

"Please, darling," he said breathlessly. "N-not here. . . ."

"The door's locked." Her smile was an evil child's. "Why don't you have a couch, like any other respectable psychiatrist?"

Price tried to maintain a certain decorum, not easily done with a beautiful woman in his lap, but he managed to say, "Do you, uh, have . . . any questions about . . . how, uh, the implant's going to work?"

She slipped her tapering fingers behind his head, pressing his face into her generous bosom, stroking his hair. "Well . . . I'm going to have a better sense of right and wrong. . . . You know, no man ever thought I needed implants before. . . ."

"I can believe that," he said. "Uh, anyway, you'll have more normal emotional responses. . . ."

She shifted her bottom in his lap. "Like you?"

"Y-yes." And gently he put his hands on her waist and lifted her off his lap. She stood there straightening herself as he asked, "Do you have the address of that halfway house?"

She nodded. "Two years seems like such a long time. . . ."

"It's not as long as being dead. Dead lasts forever."

"Thank you for sharing this medical breakthrough."

He ignored that. "And you have a car?"

Another nod, and she moved back behind him, restlessly poking at the shelves of knickknacks and books. "Neal arranged that. And he's arranged a sort of allowance, from a trust fund, within the 'parameters of the terms of my release.' . . . I feel like such a child."

"For the time being, you are. And the state is your parent—and a very strict parent at that."

Then she was behind him again, her hands on the back of his chair, rocking it, in a manner that really was childlike. So was the warmth, the pleasure in her voice as she asked, "What about my daughter? How often can I see my daughter?"

He had been dreading this question. He had withheld this dire news from her, and had seen to it that he was the messenger. He had been afraid that she might have jeopardized her release with an inflamed response in front of an official board.

Swallowing, bracing himself, he said, as gently as he could, "You . . . you can't."

In a millisecond, her warmth was gone, replaced by cold fury, and she shook the chair; it damn near sent him flying.

"What?"

She moved around to the side of the desk and faced him accusingly, her eyes wild, her nostrils flaring, her teeth bared.

He patted the air. "I . . . I really wanted to give that implant a chance to start mellowing you out before—"

She leaned into him and her rage was as if the door on a blast furnace had been opened onto him. "What do you mean, I can't see my daughter? She's my *daughter*!"

"Your sister has obtained a court order—a restraining order. . . ."

"My sister! That bitch. What *sort* of restraining order?"

"You're not to see Jessica Ann."

Her eyes were wide with indignation. "My own daughter?"

"Do I have to remind you that evidence suggesting you attempted your daughter's life was part of what led to your conviction?"

"But I would never harm her! I love Jessica Ann!"

"I know you do."

"Looking into her face was like looking into a mirror." Her smile was tortured, her laugh strident, as she gestured to her bosom. "Do you think I would harm *myself*?"

"No." And as a psychiatrist, this he knew, if he could be sure of nothing else about his patient.

She turned away from him, walked to the window, and stared at the closed blinds, rubbing her left forearm, where the implant lay snuggled beneath her flesh.

Price rose and stood behind her and put his hands on her shoulders and whispered, his words partly those of a doctor, partly those of a lover.

"I'm sorry, darling. In time, maybe we can turn that around. Talk to Ekhardt . . . he'll explain how you can best go about this. . . ."

She was slumping. Breathing hard.

He asked, "Are you all right?"

Her voice was tiny and cracked as she said, "I . . . I think so."

Price, astounded, asked, "Are you . . . crying?"

And he turned her to him and Mrs. Sterling's face, that cold, supposed sociopath's mask, was streaked with tears.

"Oh, John," she said, and flung herself into his arms; he patted her like a child.

She was as confused by this new emotion as she was sorrowful, Price could see; he would record it in his notes when she left, posing the crucial question: Was this new medicine really working?

Or had Mrs. Sterling's considerable acting skills achieved new heights?

Chapter Six

After school, as usual, Jessica Ann Sterling, cute as a bug's ear in her pink-and-blue floral bib overalls (and knowing it) retreated to her room— her *new* room, the one in Aunt Beth and Uncle Paul's three-car-garage, neo-Colonial split-level in Mark Twain Manor—to watch TV and scarf down snack food.

The petite thirteen-year-old—her slender body not yet visibly touched by puberty—enjoyed a metabolism that allowed her such dietary indiscretions. Her aunt Beth warned her that one day her metabolism would change and Jessica Ann would either have to forgo such indulgences or risk ballooning up to the size of the pre–Weight Watchers Aunt Cindy.

But Aunt Beth had stopped short of forbidding

junk food, and since—in the other house, in Mommy's house in the Woodcreek development, the late Mr. Sterling's house—the girl had never been allowed anything that wasn't healthy and nutritious, Jessica Ann was enjoying her new-found Fritos freedom.

Unlike her room at the old house—which had been pink and frilly and Mommy's idea of the perfect kid's room (it was like sleeping in a museum exhibit)—she had been allowed to make this one somewhat her own. She had decorated the mirrored sliding doors of the closets with posters of her favorite ice skaters, and a few touches from the old house—her most cherished stuffed toys (notably her sad-eyed clown and of course her teddy bear), an array of her favorite books, her boom box and CD collection, and bedside photos of her father and of her mother in matching I ♥ frames—marked the oak-paneled, open-beamed bedroom as hers.

But Beth had shown a previously unsuspected similarity to her sister by decorating the bedroom herself, without the child's input. The woman had selected the brass double bed and its mauve and turquoise bedspread (the curtains matched) and the color-coordinated floral pastel watercolor. It was as if her aunt were looking ahead to the day when Jessica Ann would be gone and she and Uncle Paul would have an extra guest room.

The television was perched high on the wall, like a TV in a hospital room, which worked out fine, because Jessica Ann could lay back on her bed with a bowl of corn chips and a can of pop and just zone out. She usually channel-surfed, landing most frequently on Comedy Central and MTV, and it wasn't like her to watch those talk shows with the lowlife people who had even worse problems than she did.

But today was a special case.

"It's *The Jenny Rivers Show*," a chubby, painfully ebullient announcer was saying, "where *your* opinions count—and here's the first lady of daytime talk—Jen . . . neeee Rivers!"

The camera panned across the studio audience, a ragtag collection of houseswives and the unemployed, who hooted and hollered and applauded as if an immediate surprise reunion of the Beatles had just been announced.

Then the camera was on gracious, graceful Jenny Rivers herself, thanking her announcer, thanking her appreciative audience, then turning to the camera as she said, painfully earnest, "Today we have a serious, even troubling topic. . . ."

Jenny Rivers—a beautiful blond woman not unlike Mommy herself, thirty-three years of age, with similar arcs of golden hair framing features so perfect either a benevolent God or a skilled plastic surgeon had to be involved—had a way of looking right into the camera, looking right through the lens and connecting with the viewer. This intimacy had rocketed Jenny Rivers past Sally Jessy Raphael, Jerry Springer, and others of the genre. Today she wore an exquisitely tailored hot pink jacket and a black blouse over a trimly shapely figure; her gorgeous legs were sheathed in black nylons. Behind her the pastel blue of her set was like a spring sky.

"I'm sure everyone in our audience remembers the so-called 'Killer Mommy' case that so gripped the media not long ago," Jenny said.

The camera again panned the audience— *trailer trash*, the girl thought, using a term Jessica Ann had heard her mother use, though she herself had never spoken it aloud—who were nodding and murmuring among themselves, a town meeting of imbeciles considering an important issue, like whether or not fluoride in the local water indicated a communist conspiracy.

"Yesterday," Jenny continued, "the woman convicted of murdering her lover Mark Patterson was released. . . ."

And there Mark was, in a smiling outdoor snapshot, though to Jessica Ann he had been Mark Jeffries, a businessman Mommy had met at the country club, not an insurance investigator, as he had revealed to the girl at her bedside on that terrible night Mommy had burst in, saying, "Close your eyes, dear," which Jessica Ann had done, though the sound of the two gunshots had opened them again. She saw Mark sprawled on her bed, his chest splotched with red, his eyes staring upward into nothing.

". . . the woman who murdered her lover in front of her own eleven-year-old daughter," Jenny was saying, but the talk show hostess wasn't on camera, a framed family photo of Jessica Ann and Mommy was, something a news crew must have shot inside the old house, during that awful time.

Then a wedding photo of Mommy and Mr. Sterling was on screen and Jenny Rivers was mentioning that Mark had been investigating Mommy's "second husband's mysterious death."

Jenny's voice seemed to blur in Jessica Ann's ears as it played over footage (labeled NEWS FILE), mostly of Mommy, sitting in the backseat of the police car at night, cherrytop light swirling and flashing, Mommy looking dazed and disheveled, which wasn't like her mother, but then Mommy had just been dragged by the police from that junkyard where she'd chased Jessica Ann.

". . . a mother who police claim, though it was never proven, attempted to murder her own little girl, to silence her as a witness. . . ."

Some of the footage was of Jessica Ann—looking so young to herself, now—standing in front of the motel in her torn pj's, clutching her teddy bear, with Aunt Beth at her side, an arm around her, comforting her.

Then Jenny Rivers was back on screen, finishing a sentence. ". . . one of Mrs. Sterling's alleged victims—Leann Jones, a janitor at the McKinley School, who died by electrocution."

And now on the screen was a photograph of Miss Jones, in another smiling outdoor snap, and this was a smile unlike any smile Jessica Ann had ever seen on the sadistic late janitor's face. As awful a person as Miss Jones had been, Jessica Ann still felt a twinge of sick nausea, particularly when the smiling photo dissolved into news footage of the janitor's blanket-covered body being wheeled out of the school by ambulance attendants.

The responsibility for the woman's death was Jessica Ann's, or so the girl thought. Hadn't she told Mommy about the mean things Miss Jones had been saying at school?

"And we have with us today the victim's sister," the talk show hostess, back on camera, was saying, "Jolene Jones."

Now, suddenly, the TV screen revealed that, seated next to Jenny on the talk show set, were her Uncle Paul and an attractive but hard looking woman in her late twenties, with big ratted reddish brown hair, lots of makeup, and a curvy body stuffed in a sexy black cocktail dress that didn't seem at all appropriate to Jessica Ann.

So this was Jolene Jones—Jessica Ann had never met the woman, but there was a strong family resemblance between the late janitor and her sister.

Jolene Jones got lots of applause and hoots and hollers, even some wolf whistles.

"We also have as our guest, Paul Conway, noted author of numerous true-crime books, including *Choked—the Mississippi Valley Strangler*, *Conversations with Killers—True Stories of Murder for Hire*, and of course the *New York Times* best-seller, *The Mommy Murders*."

Uncle Paul smiled a little nervously, acknowledging this, though the audience's applause was polite at best. It seemed funny to think that Uncle Paul was in Chicago right now, sitting next to Jenny Rivers on the talk show set, while Jessica Ann was in Ferndale, watching.

On screen, Jenny Rivers was frowning thoughtfully, her full attention on Uncle Paul. "Mr. Conway, you're not here today so much as an expert on the case, but as a representative of Mrs. Sterling's family. You're actually *married* to the sister of this convicted murderer."

Like a stomach growling, the crowd rumbled with disapproving surprise.

"That's right, Jenny," Uncle Paul said, cheerful yet serious, with no sign he was even aware of the audience's reaction. "My wife, Beth, and I met when I was researching the case, and covering the trial. I got to know the family, including Mrs. Sterling, and I think my book . . . which is just out in paperback, by the way . . . deals compassionately with this tragedy."

"I'll tell you about tragedy, you candyass son of a *bleep*," Jolene Jones said, leaning in, getting right in Paul's face, her pretty features turning ugly. "What's tragic is my *bleep bleep* sister getting her *bleep bleep bleep*in' ass fried!"

On the edges of the set, as the audience applauded and hooted their agreement, the producer of *The Jenny Rivers Show* was seated before a monitor, listening, smiling. His name was Jerry Karmen, a good-looking thirty-year-old with sandy hair, freckles, a boyish smile and a barracuda's heart. Attending him was his assistant, Christopher Kline, twenty-three years of age, devoted to his boss in and out of bed.

"Thank God for seven-second delay!" Christopher was saying as Jolene Jones continued to spew obscenities on set.

"Thank the FCC," Jerry whispered, relishing the confrontation as if it were a fine meal. "This is *great* television. . . ."

Of course, Jessica Ann did not hear any of Jerry and Christopher's conversation. But she did hear her Uncle Paul's response to the *bleep*ing Miss Jones.

"Mrs. Sterling was never charged with that crime," he was saying with calm dignity.

Now it was the talk show hostess who was leaning in toward Paul. "But your book indicates Mrs. Sterling's probable guilt. . . ."

"Probable my *bleep*!" Jolene said, nostrils flaring. "That psycho bitch is walkin' the streets, and my sister is six feet *bleep*in' under!"

"If your sister was in fact murdered," Paul said coolly but not unkindly, turning his professional gaze upon the young woman, whose attractive face was almost comically contorted by a sneer, "and it was not an unfortunate electrical accident, as was ruled by the coroner at the inquest, then she was a blackmailer who—"

"Wait a minute, wait a minute, wait a minute—

are you sayin' she deserved to die?" Jolene demanded, eyes huge, teeth bared.

"No, no—certainly not—"

Then the woman got right in Uncle Paul's face again. "You lousy piece of New York *bleep*! You made piles of money off my poor dead sister—you're gettin' rich offa other people's tragedies—"

And the television clicked off.

Surprised, irritated, Jessica Ann turned toward where her Aunt Beth stood, just inside the bedroom doorway, the remote control aimed at the now blank screen like a weapon.

Aunt Beth, in a little white top and blue skirt she'd been exercising in, looked as much a child as Jessica Ann, if not more so, her long dark hair coming around her face and down her shoulders in twin ponytails. She looked as pretty as she was cross. A crystal pendant around Aunt Beth's neck hung like a single teardrop.

"I told you," Aunt Beth said, disappointed, "I didn't want you watching that."

Jessica Ann huffed in frustration, "I just wanted to see Paul. . . ."

Aunt Beth's mouth tightened as she sat on the edge of the bed. "*He* didn't want you watching, either, did he? You heard him say things might get out of hand—"

The girl rolled her eyes. "That's why I wanted to watch it."

"I won't have you speaking to me in that tone!"

Jessica Ann looked right at her aunt and sent

as cold a message as she could. "You're not my mother."

"No," Aunt Beth said, sending back an even colder message, though she served it up hot: "But I never tried to *kill* you, either."

This verbal slap startled the girl, and her aunt's face flushed with shame.

"I'm . . . I'm sorry," Aunt Beth said.

"It's okay," Jessica Ann shrugged. "But I'm not a little kid! I have a right to know what people are saying about me, *and* Mommy—"

Aunt Beth nodded in agreement. "And there's something else you have a right to know—it's what the court thinks about you and your mommy."

Wincing in thought, Jessica Ann sat up on the bed. "What do you mean?"

Aunt Beth selected her words carefully. "The court has decided that you and your mother shouldn't have any contact for a while."

"What?"

"Not until they're sure she's . . . better."

Jessica Ann frowned, shaking her head, stunned. "I can't even see my own mother?"

This question seemed to astound her aunt. "Do you *want* to?"

"I don't know," Jessica Ann admitted.

"That's a healthy attitude, Jessy," her aunt said.

Jessica Ann couldn't decide whether her aunt was being sarcastic or not; Beth just wasn't the same person these days. There had been a time when her aunt was the only adult she could really

talk to. Her aunt and Mark, anyway. But Mommy
had killed Mark, and Beth had changed.

Jessica Ann considered herself as being on her
own now. Her response reflected that: "Whether
I see my mother or not should be up to me, not
some judge."

Aunt Beth's expression hardened; suddenly
Jessica Ann could see the family resemblance between Mommy and her. "*I'm* your guardian now,
Jessy. Your legal parent. And frankly . . . it's up
to me."

Jessica Ann could scarcely believe what she
was hearing. "If I want to see Mommy, or talk to
her—you'd stop me?"

Aunt Beth spoke in a clipped, controlled fashion that strove for frank rationality and came
across as suppressed hysteria.

"When you're eighteen," she said, "you can decide for yourself if you want a relationship with
the woman who killed your father and stepfa-
ther."

Jessica Ann glared at her aunt, but said nothing.

"But as long as you're my responsibility," Aunt
Beth said with surprising vehemence, "I can't allow you near her."

Aunt Beth almost slammed the door on the
way out.

Then Jessica Ann switched the television back
on, coming in on Jenny taking questions from
the audience. ("How can they let that crazy
woman out after she tried to break jail, huh? An-

swer me that one.") The girl glanced at the framed I ♥ MOMMY photo at her bedside.

Great, Jessica Ann thought. *Two psycho moms. . . .*

Chapter Seven

Jessica Ann's mother did not feel like herself.

She had rarely, in her life, taken medication. Her health had always been exemplary, and with the exception of birth control pills, she could not think of a time when she had taken prescription medicine. Even aspirin and cold remedies were foreign to her; she had had the flu a grand total of twice in her life and seldom caught cold. Jessica Ann had been similarly blessed.

The only time Mrs. Sterling had ever allowed doctors to medicate her was when Jessica Ann was born, and even then, her labor had been brief, the delivery relatively easy. Anyway, her pain threshold was as high as her ability to suffer fools was low.

Now, in addition to the implant beneath the

skin of her left forearm, still red, still tender, and pumping heaven knew what into her system, she was taking two drugs prescribed by John Price, one for pain, another for inflammation.

And she felt sluggish.

It had taken her forever to check in and fill out the simple paperwork, in that dreary cluttered office here at the halfway house, Wesley House. The place was not what she'd imagined, not a private home converted into cozy apartments, but a large, sprawling dormitory with cold, cubicle-like rooms, dressed up with shabby, mismatched secondhand furniture, contributions from the Methodists who supported the facility.

Her room, on the fourth floor, could have been worse, she supposed. It was not tiny, as some she had glimpsed through open doorways clearly were. The walls were a pale, pebbled-plaster pink; here and there hung maudlin religious icons—a Jesus portrait, a rustic cross, a Lord's Prayer scroll. She did not consider herself religious—in fact, she did not believe in God, though she believed in attending church, and had taken to wearing a gold crucifix (given her as a girl by her late father, the only man she had ever truly loved) during the trial.

A kitchenette area by a window included a maple captain's table with chairs that were probably nice a dozen cigarette burns ago, under a daisy-petal swag lamp that was tacky in 1971, when it was new; the nubby brown couch folded out into her bed, which she had made up (the blankets and sheets were in the bottom drawers of the single dresser—no pillows, though). Over the couch hung an oil landscape of the Old Mill out at the state park; amateur work but pleasant enough, a reminder of one of the more soothing, picturesque areas in this dreary part of the world. A dressing screen was provided (decorated in grotesquely hand-painted flowers), since the rooms were kept unlocked and one never knew when a staff member or one of these drug addicts or criminals staying here might decide to waltz in.

Though it was only late afternoon, she had left the bed folded out; she was dead tired, and the bed, sagging though it was, bony with springs, looked too inviting (and required too much effort) to put back. She had not decided whether she would take a nap or just go to bed early—she certainly did not find the unrecognizable cooking smells wafting ominously from the cafeteria (two floors away!) at all inviting.

John, at his office today—and Dr. Stern at Oakdale—had warned her that the antipsychotic medication might slow her down, slow her thoughts even as it was (supposedly) smoothing out and "regulating" her emotional responses. . . .

How insulting, she thought, standing at the kitchenette sink, taking her medicine. How could anyone think that *she* was psychotic? Was there no justice left in this sorry excuse for a world?

But more than anything else in her life right now, Mrs. Sterling wanted her daughter back.

And, medicated or not, sluggish or no, slowed to a shadow of her former self perhaps, Jessica Ann's mother could still focus as few people could. She was about to move into a phase of her life where, for the first time, someone other than herself would be the most important person.

Still in the pink suit she'd worn to John's office, Mrs. Sterling was poised at the dresser, positioning her favorite mother-and-daughter portrait of Jessica Ann and herself by a potted plant. She turned and her eyes picked out a better place for the photo, on an end table by the folded-out couch. This and the other end table (miracle of miracles, they matched) would make good homes for various family photos (nothing of Beth, that ungrateful little bitch, or of either of her late husbands—just Mommy and daughter in a better time, in a much better place).

She rested the photo there lovingly, admiring her own loveliness and her child's, found the exact position so she could see it from bed and from elsewhere in the room, then turned away and almost bumped into somebody.

Somebody who had entered, quietly, sneaking up on her, scaring the hell out of her—which was something that had never been easy for anyone to do to Mrs. Sterling.

And yet now Mrs. Sterling clutched her bosom, gasping for breath, seeking composure, as she faced the intruder.

The woman was small, almost tiny, an attractive, well-groomed woman in her late sixties, with short, carefully coiffed hair and bright blue eyes and a smile that was a little too wide in a pretty but well-lined face. She wore a blue suit and clutched a pillow to herself, as if she had been tossed overboard and it were her life preserver.

Yet, at the same, she seemed calm, self-possessed, as she asked, "Getting settled?"

Catching her breath, keeping her distance, Mrs. Sterling said, "Y-yes. . . ."

There was something familiar about the woman; should Mrs. Sterling have recognized her from somewhere?

The woman's voice was musical, in a grandmotherly fashion. "I thought you might like a pillow, dear."

"Uh, thank you."

But the woman did not offer the pillow forward; rather she continued to clutch it.

"Are you . . ." Mrs. Sterling began, feeling caught in the awkwardness like a fly in a web. "Do you live here?"

"I'm down the hall," the older woman said with a tiny nod behind her. Her smile would have seemed friendly if it hadn't been so unrelenting. Then she laughed, melodically. "Actually, I'm part of the ruling class around here. Who checked you in? Mary?"

"Why, uh, yes. . . ."

The woman tilted her head and the smile, somehow, managed to widen. "I look familiar to you, don't I?"

"Actually . . . you do." Mrs. Sterling smiled, feeling something she rarely ever had: embarrassment. "I'm sorry. . . : It's this medication. . . . I'm not quite myself. . . ."

"I'm Mrs. Evans. I used to be your daughter's principal."

"Mrs. Evans! Of course! How silly of me. At McKinley . . ."

"Lovely child, Jessica Ann. I trust she's well?"

"Yes."

"Staying with her aunt, I understand."

"That's right."

"It must be terrible for you, separated from her like this."

"Yes. It is."

"I retired at the end of the last school year, and now I'm helping out here, at Wesley House. . . ."

"Good for you," Mrs. Sterling said with barely disguised disdain, more than ready for this guest to hand her the damn pillow and go.

"Yes," Mrs. Evans said, "isn't it? Well, dear, I just wanted to welcome you . . ."

"Thank you."

". . . and let you know I'll be watching you."

Mrs. Sterling wasn't sure she'd heard that right. "Watching?"

The smile disappeared. The woman's lined, pretty features tightened into an unpleasant, mummy-like mask. "Mrs. Withers, the teacher you killed—"

"That was never proven!"

The bright blue eyes had frozen. "—she was a

wonderful woman, a wonderful teacher, and one of my best friends."

Mrs. Sterling was shaking her head, no, no. "That was an accident. That was ruled an accident. . . ."

"I know dear," Mrs. Evans said sweetly, the smile returning, curdled though it was. "You're innocent . . . like O. J."

The words were like a physical blow. She swallowed, managed to say, "I'm just trying to—"

"I just wanted you to know that it will be my pleasure to report the slightest infraction on your part."

"You're not being fair. . . ."

"Were you fair to Thelma Withers when you pulled that ladder out from under her? Please keep in mind, dear, that nothing will give me greater satisfaction than to see you back on death row, where you belong. . . ."

And the grandmotherly woman thrust the pillow forward, smacking it into Mrs. Sterling, almost knocking her over.

"Good afternoon," Mrs. Evans said sweetly, and left, leaving the door open so that the noise of the hall, and of the TV playing in the nearby lounge, could intrude on Mrs. Sterling's privacy.

Jessica Ann's mother clutched the pillow, and turned to look at the framed portrait of her daughter and herself in happier days, in that much happier place. She felt almost woozy from the older woman's verbal attack; agitated, and yet so very tired.

And as if that weren't enough, strange emotions were churning in her; tears were in her eyes.

What had she ever done to deserve such hatred?

Chapter Eight

The Ferndale Sports Center—a huge metal barn that housed an ice-skating rink and a volleyball court—drew from the small surrounding towns and easily justified its existence with its packed-house weekend crowds. Weekdays, after school and evenings, however, the vast skating rink was sparsely populated, an ideal time for private lessons.

The next evening, out on the ice of the skating rink, Jessica Ann—in her oversize white Sports Center sweatshirt and dark stretch pants and purple leggings—glided by, as her aunt and uncle watched from the bleachers, separated from the skaters by a Plexiglas barrier.

This wasn't Jessica Ann's night for private instruction (she studied with a former Olympic skater), but she had begged her aunt and uncle to let her come to the "open skating" period between lessons. A few parents were sprinkled here and there in the stands as perhaps a dozen kids did their own thing, which ranged from graceful figure eights to ungainly pratfalls.

Jessica Ann, though a relative beginner—she'd been skating for less than six months—was one of the more graceful skaters out there. She did not try anything terribly difficult, but she had a fluid, theatrical, feminine style that promised great things.

Beth Conway was proud of her niece, impressed by her abilities, and yet even the girl's love for skating troubled her—though as concerns went, it was far, far down on the list.

"I think you're dead wrong about this, Beth," Paul said. He had brought along a lightweight ivory sweater to fling over a blue sports shirt; his sports shirt was right for the May weather outside, though the artificial winter in here required the sweater.

Beth had dressed warm, too, a canary windbreaker over her white blouse, but she was cold. So was her reply: "I'm not going to have Jessy anywhere *near* that woman."

Jessica Ann was doing a little jump as she turned; she wasn't just goofing around out there, rather practicing specific moves.

"Personally," Paul said, "I think it would be good for both of them."

Beth shot him a bitter look. "Good?"

Paul nodded. "They both have a lot of healing to do—and the sooner they start, the better."

"That's easy for you to say," Beth said with a humorless laugh. She hugged herself, shivering. "You're not the one who walked away from that little girl and left her in the care of a sociopath."

They had been down this road before, many times, and Beth knew it, but couldn't help herself.

"Beth, please, don't beat yourself up over this anymore." He touched her sleeve. "There was nothing you could have done. Anyway, you had no legal right—"

She shook her head, no, and held her head high. "I had a moral responsibility. I *knew* my sister was potentially dangerous, and yet I left that child in harm's way because I was too afraid to stand up to her! Well . . . I'm not afraid now."

Paul's response was reasonable, but firm: "I don't want to argue about it, Beth. . . . Beth! Look at me. Please."

She sighed, and did.

He said, "I'm just expressing an opinion. . . . I'm Jessy's legal guardian too, remember."

She loved this man so. His gentleness. His insight. Those gray-blue eyes could melt her. But she would not give in to him on this. Her sister must be kept away from Jessica Ann. Even the courts were on her side.

Still, Paul was right: There was no reason for them to get at each other over this.

"I know," she said. "I'm sorry."

93

That made Paul smile, and he leaned forward and gave her a peck, which made her smile, too.

Out on the ice, by herself (unlike many of the kids, she did not skate with a partner), Jessica Ann was skating fast now, moving into a wide, gliding arc, arms spread as if presenting herself to the world.

"You know," Paul said, "for a beginner, she's really very good. She's got real poise. And a certain flair. I think she's going to do very well in competition."

Beth shook her head. "I don't know if this is so good for her."

This caught her husband by surprise. "What, are you crazy?"

But Beth was serious, her eyes fixed upon her niece, out there lost in her skating. "I mean, every day, she pressures us to bring her here, to practice."

"And just about every day, we give in to her. So?"

"Well don't you think she's overdoing it a little? That she's gotten . . . obsessed with this skating?"

He slipped his arm around her shoulder. "It can be healthy to have obsessions. Like, for instance, how I'm obsessed with you . . ."

And he kissed her again, melting her, even if her teeth were chattering.

"Anyway, Jessica Ann needs something in her life," he said, "something positive, something to distract her. I mean, let's face it, she has problems few girls her age face."

Beth smirked. "Like having a homicidal maniac for a mother?"

"That does set her apart," he admitted wryly. He nodded out toward the girl, who was coming to a kneeling, ice-spraying stop. "Now, this skating—it's healthy."

"Maybe if she were meeting other kids . . . but she's such a loner. . . ."

"Nothing wrong with that. She was sheltered for a long time. Don't forget—as intelligent as she is, she was also . . . stunted by her mother's smothering attention. When I first met Jessica Ann, she was, what? Eleven?"

"Eleven," Beth confirmed.

"Well, in many respects, she behaved like a seven-or eight-year-old. Of course, in other ways, she had a maturity you don't find in many adults."

"So what are you saying?"

"Give her a chance to catch up with the other kids . . . and with herself. Developing a new interest like this, like skating, something she didn't do when she was living with her mother, it's a new beginning for her."

She touched his hand. "Paul—what would I do without you?"

He grinned at her. "Some foolish damn thing. Ah! Here comes Nancy Kerrigan now."

Jessica Ann was skating up to the Plexiglas barrier, where she came to a stop with a bump and a comical false cry of pain; her aunt and uncle were seated in the third row with no one seated on the bleachers between them and the barrier, so the three only had to raise their voices a little to converse through the Plexi.

Beth asked, "You about ready to go, Jessy?"

"Can't I stay a while?" the girl asked. She glanced toward the hockey scoreboard clock. "Lessons don't start till six."

Beth looked at Paul. "Another forty-five minutes?"

He shrugged. "Why not?" he said to his wife, almost whispering. "Why don't we slip out of here and pick those groceries up?"

"Good idea," Beth said to her husband, then to her niece she called, "Sure, sweetie! We'll pick you up then."

The girl gestured to herself theatrically. "Aren't you going to watch me some more?"

This tiny burst of self-confidence, of self-esteem from the girl, raised a surge of warmth within Beth. Paul was right. The skating was good for her.

Paul called out to Jessica Ann, "No, honey—it's too cold for us non-Eskimos! See you at six."

The child smirked at her uncle's silly joke, waved, and skated off. Beth and Paul, on their way out, paused and watched the girl gliding across the ice, dancing on the toes of her skates with ballerina grace. Then they waved one last time and exited.

But after her uncle and aunt had left, Jessica Ann—though she didn't know it—still had an audience.

Someone was standing under the stands, hidden there, peeking out with haunted china-blue eyes between the bleacher boards as her daughter sailed by on gleaming silver skates.

Chapter Nine

"You didn't *talk* to her?" Dr. Price asked, alarmed by his patient's admission of her visit to the Ferndale Sports Center. "You didn't actually make contact with your daughter . . . ?"

Seated in Price's office near his desk as the psychiatrist sat perched on the edge of it, Mrs. Sterling—touching her gold cross on its gold chain as it bisected the modest V neck of her pale pink cardigan, which rode the top of her full, long, floral-print skirt—said, "No. I . . . I just watched." Then, with trembling martyrdom, she added, "From afar."

It was evening. The private offices of Towncrest Medical Center were closed, Price's included, but when Mrs. Sterling had called him at home, he had suggested they come here. They had met in the parking lot and he had used various keys to admit them into the darkened building. He felt only a little guilty at the elation he felt at the promise of a rendezvous with his beautiful patient, with whom he had spent no intimate time since her release.

Price's marriage had been a strained truce for several years, since Mary Ann had discovered that her husband had been having a relationship with one of his patients (not Mrs. Sterling). He had promised her it would never happen again, and Mary Ann—for the sake of the children (and their house and reputations and an affluent ongoing life)—had agreed to stay with him. They occasionally had sexual relations, and were politely friendly to each other. But there was no laughter, no love in the marriage. And he was convinced Mary Ann would divorce him this time, if she learned he'd resumed his "ways."

Like most doctors, Price could not heal himself, and in fact rationalized his behavior as both normal and acceptable. He had been in only a handful of intimate relationships with female patients, and felt that in every case he had improved their conditions through his loving therapy.

Mrs. Sterling was no exception. What doctor could have accomplished more for a patient than Price had for her? Hadn't he saved her life?

And, anyway, he was seduced, not seducer—back at Oakdale, hadn't she made the advances toward him?

Now, here she was in his office, looking lovelier than ever, so softly pretty, almost glowing in attire far more feminine than the severe suits she was known to wear, the outline of her bosom under the pink cardigan fetching to say the least. The sweater was certainly more attractive than a shapeless orange prison uniform. . . .

But Price put his patient's welfare before his own gratification and interests. His first concern, tonight, was to find out what was troubling Mrs. Sterling.

She had sounded most distraught on the phone; and far more emotional than he had ever heard her before.

Sighing, looming above her as he sat perched on the desk, he said firmly, "If you'd been seen spying on Jessica Ann, you'd have caused yourself a world of trouble. You're violating a court order."

Her mouth tensed into a tight line, her eyes avoided his. "I wasn't spying on her."

"Your sister would call it that. She'd probably call it *stalking*."

A tiny sneer distorted her mouth. "She's the sick one."

"You may be right."

She gazed up at him yearningly; with her hands folded in her lap, she looked like a sad, pitiful child. But a lovely one.

"I want to do more than just . . . see Jessica Ann. I want to talk to her. I need to talk to her."

Price shook his head, no, though he didn't even

try to hide the reluctance behind his words. "I can't encourage you to talk to her, much as I might personally think it's a healthy thing."

Her eyes were wide with hurt and indignation. "What's wrong with a mother talking to her daughter?"

"Don't you understand? You're endangering your outpatient status!"

A humorless smirk dimpled a pretty cheek. "My 'outpatient status.'"

"Yes."

"You mean, I'll get thrown back on to death row," she huffed bitterly; but there was weariness in her tone, too.

"Yes," Price said solemnly. "There are a lot of people who would like nothing better than to see you fail."

"Really?" Mrs. Sterling said archly. "I hadn't noticed."

He frowned, leaned forward. "Have you had . . . problems? With Beth?"

"No. I haven't had any contact with her, or her husband."

Then she told him of her confrontation with Mrs. Evans at the halfway house. In general, she had not been received warmly at Wesley House, either by staff or fellow "inmates," as she put it.

"You're not an inmate."

"What would you call it?"

"You're a resident. You can come and go as you please. . . ."

"Signing in and out."

"Is that so bad?"

She shrugged.

"Do you want me to try to get you transferred to another halfway house? If Mrs. Evans is going to present a problem, we can—"

"No." She shook her head, blond hair shimmering, and looked up at him with china-blue eyes that brimmed with self-pity. "Do you really think a change of venue would matter, in a case this notorious? No. No, thank you."

He looked at her, her head bowed in defeat, a posture he had never imagined he would see from this woman, and felt a rush of sympathy for her. No matter what she had done, she was a mother who loved her daughter; the medication was unleashing genuine emotions in her, for perhaps the first time in her life, and the state was refusing to allow her to act upon them.

Leaning forward, still above her, he plucked a hand from her lap and held it in both of his, patting her soothingly.

He said, "You know, don't you, that I would do anything within my power for you. . . ."

She gazed at him; the blue eyes suddenly became beseeching laser beams that bored through his skull. "Then help me get my daughter back!"

He shook his head in frustration. "No, custody is out of the question—"

"Not custody," she said. "I know that's hopeless right now. . . . I just want to see her, to talk to her. . . ." She leaned forward, tears glistening but not quite falling. "I want Jessica Ann not to hate me. . . ."

"I'm sure she doesn't hate you—"

"I need to know that. And she needs to know I love her!" Then her expression of tortured tenderness dissolved into a more familiar, hateful mask. "I just know Beth." She spoke her sister's name as if spitting out a distasteful seed. "I know she's saying terrible, hurtful things. . . ."

He stroked her hand. Smiled down at her reassuringly. "Look. Keep your pretty little nose clean, and who knows? With my help, and Ekhardt's—and you know you have that, don't you?—in six months, maybe a year . . ."

And he leaned in to kiss her.

But it didn't happen: She pulled away, almost recoiled.

He blinked, then drew away a few inches. "Is something wrong?"

"Please . . ."

He touched her face. "We're safe here. Alone . . . or would you rather we went somewhere else?"

She removed his hand from her cheek as if she were lifting off a scab.

"Darling . . . what's wrong?"

Mrs. Sterling straightened herself, smoothing her sweater, her flowing skirt; suddenly very prim and proper, she looked at him innocently and said, "I just don't . . . I just don't feel that way about you anymore, Doctor."

He felt as though he'd been struck a physical

blow; nausea flowed through his stomach. "Oh," he said.

She cocked her head, and her expression was a peculiar mixture of worry and assurance. "Is that going to be a problem?"

"No," he said, and his face felt like putty, as if his every feature would slide off into a blobby puddle at his feet. Then he summoned the will to smile, just a little, and said, "No, not at all . . ."

And Dr. John Price suddenly realized that his treatment was working. He was winning the battle for this patient, even if he had lost a lover.

"Pull your sleeve back," he told her clinically. "And let's have a look at that arm, see how that implant's doing. . . ."

She drew back the cardigan's sleeve to reveal the bump under the skin; the swelling had gone down, the redness was fading. It was as much of her sweet body as he would see that night.

Chapter Ten

In her room in the Conways' Mark Twain Manor home that night, in white cotton pajamas adorned with pink flowers—jammies that her mommy had bought her before the trouble—Jessica Ann sat reading an R. L. Stine thriller, a book her mother would no doubt have forbidden her to read.

Her homework was complete—old habits die hard, and she was still the perfect, well-behaved student her mother had raised her to be—and she was fighting sleepiness, tired from the several hours of skating. But she wanted to see how the story came out, and relished her ability to stay up later than her mother would have allowed.

Her life was like that now—a peculiar mix of behavior drilled into her by her mother that butted up against the more permissive parenting style of Beth and Paul, the bits and pieces of the old life (like her teddy bear in its green dress gazing forlornly at her from atop the dresser) and the new (her mother would never have allowed the distraction of television in her daughter's room).

Consequently, Jessica Ann was moving from childhood into adolescence in a state of confusion, a limbo that kept her off balance, typified by her aunt's conduct of late, which veered from being far more lenient than Mommy ever had been to recent outbursts which forbade the girl from even speaking to her own mother.

When she referred to her mother aloud, the girl would say, "My mother"; but to herself the woman who raised her remained forever "Mommy," childish as that might be. That cold night in the junkyard, under a black-streaked moon, their relationship had been frozen in amber, and though Jessica Ann had grown older, her relationship with her mother remained fixed. Perhaps, where Mommy was concerned, Jessica Ann would always be eleven years old.

Or six.

She was just nodding off, the book faltering in her hands, when the knock at her door woke her. "Yes?"

Uncle Paul cracked the door and peeked in. His smile warmed her. "Got a second, pal?"

"Sure," Jessica Ann said, marking her place in the book and setting it aside. "Come on in."

Uncle Paul looked casual and yet neat as a *GQ* ad in his blue denim shirt and new jeans; he reminded the girl of the late Mark Jeffries, or Patterson, who had the same sort of soap opera–star handsome features and dark hair touched with distinguished premature gray.

Uncle Paul had the same gentle manner with the girl as well, and spoke in a similarly soothing baritone.

Reflexively, the girl glanced at the picture of her late father in the I ♥ DADDY frame; Daddy had a rugged, outdoorsy look, and in the snapshot was on his boat, proudly displaying a fish he'd caught. This was the same boat Daddy had fallen off of and drowned when he was out with Mommy that time.

Though she had never quite let Mr. Sterling into her heart—nice though he was, he had seemed more a grandfather than a father to her—Jessica Ann had seriously hoped, after Mr. Sterling had died, that Mark would be her new daddy. It didn't work out, what with Mommy shooting him instead of marrying him, but now Jessica Ann finally had her new dad, in the form of Uncle Paul, and with the weird way Aunt Beth had been acting, she was very relieved to have him, to have any stable, caring adult in her life.

He settled on the edge of the bed, a respectful distance from the girl, who said, "I saw you on TV yesterday."

He had gotten back from Chicago this afternoon—he had driven into the city (it was only a three-hour trip) but stayed overnight to do more "media business"—and this was the first time Jessica Ann had been alone with him, to discuss the subject.

"You did, huh?"

"Till Beth shut it off," she elaborated.

"Yeah," he said, shaking his head, his half grin almost embarrassed. "So I heard. . . . Beth's a little uptight about all this."

Jessica Ann laughed. "You think?"

His grin widened. "Well, you have to admit, things did get kinda wild."

She made a distasteful face. "That Jolene Jones is an awful woman."

"She's no better in person. I didn't know they were going to pair me up with her; I would've refused to go on."

"They didn't tell you?"

"No." He sighed. "I won't make the mistake of going on *Jenny Rivers* again. The producers are a bunch of liars, just looking to throw their 'guests' into confrontations."

"Why do they do that?"

"Ratings. People like to watch that sort of thing."

"Why?"

"Who knows? But it goes back to the Romans tossing the Christians to the lions."

The girl nodded. "I bet that would get good ratings, too."

"I bet you're right," he chuckled. "So . . . maybe you can see that your aunt was right, in her way—that show wasn't really anything you needed to see."

"It didn't upset me. I'm not stupid. I'm not six."

"I know. I know." He was patting the air with both palms, as if surrendering to her. "Let's not us have a confrontation."

She laughed a little. "Yeah, let's not."

"Look, pal . . . where your Aunt Beth's concerned, with your mommy and everything?"

"Yes, Paul?"

"Do me a favor?"

"Well . . . I'll try."

"Good. Cut her a little slack."

Jessica Ann folded her arms and leaned back against the brass headboard. She turned her eyes away as she said to him, "You know what she told me?"

"What did she tell you?"

Now she looked right at him. "That I can't see Mommy, or talk to her, or anything—*ever*."

That seemed to amuse Paul, just a little. Gently teasing, he said, "Ever?"

"Well . . . same as. Till I'm eighteen."

"Ah," Uncle Paul said, and then his smile disappeared. His expression was serious, but not stern. "I happen to think you're right to want to understand and forgive your mommy. . . ."

Hope rushed through the girl, and she sat up, rustling the sheets, eyes bright. "Really?"

"Really."

"Well, then . . ." Her mind was swimming with possibilities. "Why can't we . . . you know, invite her over or something? And just see how she's doing?"

Uncle Paul smiled again, but it was a sad smile, and he studied her for a long time before saying, "You miss her?"

Duh.

"She is my mother," Jessica Ann said.

He swallowed and again he looked at her for a long time before he spoke. He seemed to be talking more to himself than to Jessica Ann, now. "Someday I'll get you two back together . . . I promise. Till then—will you promise *me* something?"

Feeling almost chipper now, she asked, "What, Paul?"

"Promise me you'll put up with this, this . . . commandment of your aunt's, about not seeing your mother. Do that for me, now—and I'll work on later."

That was the moment when Jessica Ann decided she loved her Uncle Paul, and accepted him as the father figure she so desperately needed.

"Okay," she whispered.

His eyes were tight, but they were filled with kindness. "Your aunt knows that you love her. But she needs more. She needs your respect."

Genuinely puzzled by this remark, Jessica Ann asked, "Why, Paul?"

"Because she hasn't really learned to respect herself yet," he said, and as she tried to absorb that thought, he rose and, at the door, paused to say, "G'night, pal."

She beamed at him. "G'night."

From the doorway he gave her a thumbs-up, and the girl returned it.

Tired now, she put her book on the nightstand, taking time only to carefully adjust the two framed photos at her bedside, I ♥ MOMMY, I ♥ DADDY, her eyes lingering on the smiling bearded face of her late father.

Then she turned off the light and, for the first time in a long time, went right to sleep.

Chapter Eleven

At one end of the skating rink at Ferndale Sports Center, Jessica Ann was working with her instructor, while on the rest of the ice open skating was under way.

For early evening, attendance was pretty good, perhaps two dozen young skaters whose movements, consciously or not, were affected by the rhythm of the early-'60s bubblegum rock number blaring distortedly over the sound system ("No, she can't find her keys!"), bouncing and echoing around the cavernous, cold chamber. A sprinkling of parents were in the stands, as usual, but Jessica Ann's aunt and uncle were not among them; they would pick the girl up at seven, after her lesson.

Her blond hair in a bouncing ponytail, the

girl's pretty, slender legs flashed under the short skirt of the cute little turquoise skating outfit. With her aunt's blessing, she had picked the dress out herself—she could never imagine Mommy approving so short a skirt—to wear in the competition next month.

Her instructor, Matt Sharp, reminded Jessica Ann of Luke Skywalker, except Matt dressed more like Darth Vader—black sweatshirt, black stretch pants, even a black baseball cap, which Jessica Ann had never seen Matt without. He was a terrific skater—he'd competed at the '92 Olympics—and was really good at giving encouragement and sharing little tips and tricks. He taught by example, showing her moves and then having her imitate them.

"Keep at that axel," he told her, before skating over to help one of the other three students sharing this instruction period, "and you're gonna do fine next week."

She worked on the axel and other bits and pieces of her routine, which concluded with a graceful spin that turned her pretty little dress into a turquoise blur. At the end of the twirl, she came to a graceful, posed stop, her arms spread in "ta da!" fashion.

But her practiced performance smile first froze, then cracked, as she saw a familiar face, poised at the Plexiglas barrier. The child looked around the arena, as if seeking the advice of someone, anyone, and seeing only the looming advertising signs, the displayed American and

Canadian flags near the scoreboard, laughing, yelping, hollering kids skating by in smears of motion, and the indistinct faces of the handful of spectators in the stands—a big, empty world, full of all sorts of things, but not help.

Even Matt was busy.

In the area between the two tiers of bleachers, with the doorway to the arena lobby behind her, stood a beautiful woman with arcs of icy blond hair, watching the skaters. Or anyway, one skater.

Jessica Ann swallowed and skated closer.

It was Mommy, all right.

She looked very pretty, in a silk blouse so pale a pink it seemed at first white, the cross on its necklace worn on the outside, light from the hanging lamps high above winking off the gold, making tiny dancing crosses. Mommy was touching the smudgy, scratched Plexi with one hand and the smile on her face conveyed both pride and yearning.

Jessica Ann glided slowly up to the Plexiglas barrier, and came to an abrupt, ice-screeching stop. The girl folded her red-cotton-gloved hands where the windows met the metal wall, unconsciously mimicking the prayer-like position of her mother's hands, resting on the other side of the Plexi. With the wall of plastic between them, it was like visitor's day at a prison; however, who the visitor was, and who the prisoner was, was uncertain.

"You look so beautiful out there," Mommy

said, raising her voice a little; the Plexi made that necessary. "So graceful . . ."

"I asked you once if I could take lessons," the girl said guardedly, head lowered, eyes raised, "and you said it was too dangerous."

"Your mother made some mistakes, dear," Mommy admitted with a nervous nod.

Jessica Ann looked from side to side; fortunately, no one's eyes were on them. "You know we're not supposed to talk."

Gently, Mommy asked, "Do you really think that's anyone's business but ours?"

It wasn't really a question.

"No," Jessica Ann said, answering it anyway, just as gently. "But I don't want to get either one of us in trouble."

Mommy smiled thinly. "Your Aunt Beth told you not to talk to me, didn't she?"

Jessica Ann swallowed, nodded. "But it's more than that. You know what she did."

Mommy nodded, too. "I know about the court order. But I'm not bothering you. I'm just watching."

The girl's eyes widened, as she again looked around to see if anyone had noticed them. "We're talking!"

Mommy swallowed; she seemed hurt. "Do you . . . do you want me to leave?"

The girl thought about that, then said, "No . . . but you'd better anyway."

Mommy beamed at that, apparently able to ignore the second part of the response, and, with false cheer, asked, "How are you doing in school?"

Jessica Ann's shrug was barely perceptible. "Okay, I guess."

"Seventh grade," Mommy sighed. She was shaking her head, and her smile was sad and happy at once. "My little girl is growing up. . . . You look so pretty in that dress."

"It is a little short."

"Your legs are getting so long. You'll be taller than your mommy before you know it. . . ." A thought danced in Mommy's eyes. "What about your grades? Any B's?"

"No. Just A's."

And that prompted another thought, really perking Mommy up. "Are they giving an Outstanding Student Award . . . ?"

"No!" The girl's eyes popped wide in alarm. "They stopped doing that."

After Mrs. Withers died.

Jessica Ann moved away a little. "I have to go. . . . I'm kind of in the middle of a private lesson. . . ."

"I'm proud of you!" Mommy called as her daughter began to move away.

But the girl almost bumped into Matt Sharp, skating over; his boyish features had a cold blankness that Jessica Ann knew meant her generally easygoing instructor was irritated about something. She froze in place as he streaked by her, ice-spraying to a stop.

"Excuse me!"

Mommy was backing up, startled, and Matt opened the nearly invisible door in the Plexi barrier and leaned through it, until he was almost in the woman's face.

"You're Mrs. Sterling, aren't you? Jessica Ann's mother?"

Mommy smiled hesitantly. "Why, yes. . . ."

Matt turned to Jessica Ann and said, "Jessica Ann, do me a favor—go practice that axel for a while, would you?"

"Okay," she nodded. "Bye, Mommy."

"Good-bye, dear! Practice hard!"

And the girl skated out, away from them, but she didn't practice. She stood and watched and, positioning herself where she knew the voices would carry, listened.

"Parental interest is something I encourage," Matt said.

Mommy smiled some more, but she seemed anxious. "I'm . . . I'm glad to hear that."

"*Normally* I encourage it," Matt said. "But I know all about you, Mrs. Sterling."

"Now, this isn't fair. . . ."

"And I know about the restraining order."

Mommy was shaking her head as if Matt didn't understand. "I just wanted to watch my little girl skate. . . ."

"Jessica Ann is in training, Mrs. Sterling," Matt said sternly, "for her first competition."

"I know. . . ."

"And she doesn't need this kind of pressure."

If Jessica Ann didn't know her mother better,

she would have sworn Mommy was on the verge of tears. "I . . . I wasn't hurting anything."

Matt's tone was matter-of-fact, and yet menacing. "I don't want to see you around here again. Understood?"

"But—"

"If I do, I'll report you."

And Matt yanked the door closed, slamming it, startling Mommy again, and skated away.

Mommy, trembling, frustrated, agitated, called out to him, nearly screaming, "But she's my *daughter*!"

Mommy's voice echoed through the vast arena, *daughter daughter daughter*, a reverberating cry bouncing off the metal rafters and demanding attention, and Matt turned, skating backward, arms folded, saying nothing, gazing at her contemptuously.

Other eyes were on her, too, from the nearby stands, as people recognized the notorious woman and began to whisper and point and stare—some of them would report that Mrs. Sterling had seemed embarrassed, others would recall an ice-cold expression as if rage were bubbling within the woman, barely controlled.

Jessica Ann, petrified out on the ice, looked toward her mother with pity and concern, wanting to do something, but Mommy—wrapping herself in her own humiliation, as if it were a protective cloak—scurried out into the night before her daughter could offer so much as a word of solace.

Chapter Twelve

By 9 P.M. the Ferndale Sports Center was closed, and by 9:15 every parent and even the last stray kid was out the door, skates and jackets slung over shoulders as the chilly arena was traded for a gently breezy May evening, dusk barely turning to night.

The big arena squatted alongside highway 61 on the north edge of town, near the new Wal-Mart and Menard's superstores and the sprawling Hy-Vee grocery superstore that were helping turn the nearby Ferndale Mall into a ghost town. These metal monoliths crouched along the busy stretch of highway, monuments to mammon, pyramids of modern times.

The parking lots of its superstore neighbors were packed, but the Ferndale Sports Center lot was nearly empty—just the janitor's beat-up blue Ford pickup and Head Instructor Matt Sharp's white Camaro, and one other car, a red Sunbird, which did not belong to anyone employed at the facility.

In fact, janitor Casper Scott noticed the Sunbird in the lot when he checked the outer lobby for stragglers at 9:20; but heavyset, mustached Scott had shrugged that off, displaying the go-getter disposition that had, at age thirty-eight, won him a part-time maintenance man job that he was one warning away from losing.

Scott was to get off at ten, and at a quarter to, when the burly janitor—in his jeans and heavy khaki shirt—went back into the big chilly skating rink to take a quick pass through the stands with his Glad bag–lined can, picking up candy wrappers and discarded cups and such, he found the lights in the arena were largely off. This did not surprise him—actually, it was typical, when that arrogant show-off Sharp was working.

Tonight, as was so often the case, Sharp had lighted up the vast icy floor of the rink with occasional spotlights, yellowish pools of light for him to glide into and through as he used the entire arena for his own practice and pleasure.

Scott considered this pitiful. Everybody knew the instructors here were washed up, a bunch of ice-skating has-beens too old for the Olympics, not good enough for "Holiday on Ice" and other travelling shows. And there was Sharp, travelling from one spotlight to another, emerging from the darkness into the circles of light, jumping and whirling and spinning.

What a loser, Scott thought, as he crouched to pick up a half-eaten hot dog to place in the garbage can.

The janitor was wrong about Sharp, who was a gifted skater and could easily have worked the ice-show circuit; in fact, Matt had starred as the Beast in Disney's *Beauty and the Beast* touring company (though the heat and weight of the bulky beast costume had damn near killed him) and had a standing offer from the Disney people, who always had some ice show or another touring.

But Matt and his young wife—also an instructor here, a former Olympian from Moscow—had wanted to settle down, and this was an opportunity to pursue a career in skating and at the same time lead a more normal life, here in the all-American heartland where the cost of living was low, and so was the crime rate. Olga was expecting and Matt would be a father before too long.

Still, skating was his first love, and the joy of having all this ice to himself, to keep his skills honed, to enjoy the sheer masculine pleasure of the jumps and spins, feeling the power of his legs as he streaked across the ice, was one of the best perks of a job marred only by the occasional pain-in-the-ass "stage mother" and other unreasonable parents an instructor encountered in this very competitive sport.

It was worse than Little League, all the petty bickering. Matt by nature was easygoing, laid-back even (he was a California native and there was a touch of the surfer in him, even if he did prefer his water frozen) but he had cultivated a reputation among the moms (and dads, but in skating, which was for the most part girls, it was mostly moms) so that they would steer clear of him. Word among the parents was: Don't cross Matt Sharp, and these days they rarely did.

Today he had let that Sterling woman have it, and though she herself had been docile enough, he had read the papers, he had seen the media, he knew who this woman was. Jessica Ann, beginner though she was, had great potential; she had a flair, a showmanship and even a blossoming self-confidence that could set her apart. He wasn't about to let her sick psychopath mother ruin that; he wasn't afraid of that bitch. He liked Jessica Ann and wanted only the best for her; this first competition could be crucial.

From the stands, that lazy bastard of a janitor called out to him, "Hey!"

"Yeah?" Matt said, gliding into the pool of light nearest the Plexiglas barrier behind which the janitor was halfheartedly gathering refuse from the stands.

The janitor's expression was one of disgust and irritation; but then, that was usually the case. "How long you gonna work out in here, anyway?"

"About an hour or so," Matt said, sailing by.

"Hour or so," Scott muttered, grunting as he

picked up a Snickers wrapper and tossed it into his can. He called out to Matt, who was halfway down the ice, "Turn out the lights yourself, then!"

And as the janitor, grumbling, moved down the stadium steps, he did not notice (nor did the skating Sharp) that someone was standing under the stands, hidden there, peeking out from behind designer sunglasses from between the bleacher boards, watching the skating instructor skate, so beautifully, in the otherwise empty arena.

Casper Scott had left the building by the time the blond woman came out from under the stands; dressed in a severe yet feminine blue suit, with nylons and black spike heels, she might have been attending a country club luncheon. She was holding something behind her back, as if about to approach a child and present a surprise gift.

Her heels made tiny clicks on the cement as she skirted the edge of the ice-skating rink, moving to one of the doors in the Plexi barrier, then opening it, and striding out onto the glassy surface of the ice in high heels, walking as casually, as naturally, as if she were moving out onto a ballroom's polished dance floor—yes, it was slick, and one had to be careful, but it was maneuverable enough. She moved with ease onto the ice, well out onto it in fact, with no more trouble than Christ walking on water.

Matt Sharp was lost in his routine, landing jumps, achieving just the desired placement, drilling himself as he did his students, *pull those arms in, check strong on that jump, stand it up*, a double axel, even a triple, spinning into a blur of black and silver, his skates flashing.

Then he saw the rather petite, slender, shapely blond woman standing on the ice, impeccably attired in the blue suit. It was a startling sight, a living misnomer, and bizarre at that: sunglasses at night, here in this dark arena?

Was that Jessica Ann's mother?

Anger rose in him, and he snugged his baseball cap in place (never without it, his brown hair thinning slightly) and skated swiftly across the expansive ice toward her, stopping right next to her, spraying her high heels, though she didn't rear back, rather standing her ground.

"What the hell are you doing here?" he demanded of the blond woman. He gestured toward the door forcefully, a slap that didn't connect. "Get off the ice!"

That was when Matt noticed that the blond woman was holding something behind her back, which she now withdrew; in a graceful hand with perfect red-painted nails, the woman held a hockey skate, which Matt immediately recognized as belonging to the Sports Center, simple for the woman to have grabbed from behind the counter out in the lobby.

When the blond woman raised the skate in a motion that was like the throwing of a switch, she held it upside down, blade up, the heel of the skate forward, silver steel winking and gleaming and flashing in the spotlight, the woman gripping it as if it were a weapon—which it was. Matt raised a hand reflexively and the first slashing blow cut a deep bloody groove in his left palm. The next slash cut a gaping crevice in his cheek, which would have left a nasty scar had he lived through what followed.

As his blood wept red teardrops onto the ice, Matt Sharp did not even cry out; he did not think to—he was too busy getting slashed to ribbons, his other cheek gashed and gaping, his championship feet struggling in the skates to keep his balance on the blood-spattered ice under this calmly delivered, yet relentless onslaught of slashing blows, from the right, from the left, and then he was losing his balance, and as he tipped forward she clutched the skate in both hands and delivered a bullfighter-like coup de grâce that slammed him dead to the ice, even as she stepped gracefully aside.

That Matt Sharp was dead did not dissuade the blond woman from continuing; she knelt over the face-down splayed body of the instructor, hammering the spike-like heel of the skate blade into his back again and again, as blood streamed from Sharp's body, staining the ice, soaking into it, adding color to the pool of light, the circle of attention that victim and killer shared, though without an audience.

Matt Sharp—who would never see his child—died with his baseball cap snugged over his thinning hair, a modicum of decorum for a well-tuned, highly trained athlete whose body had been cut and gouged to pieces. Easygoing Matt Sharp—in his final performance, in the spotlight—would now forever be spared of the indignity of dealing with some girl skater's pain-in-the-ass stage mother.

Chapter Thirteen

On his way to Wesley House to see Mrs. Sterling, Sergeant Max Anderson dropped by to see his retired partner. It was early afternoon and—on the blindingly white sunporch of March's wealthy wife's modern white near mansion—the former detective sat in his wheelchair in a Hawaiian sports shirt and loose-fitting chinos and sandals, facing a well-tended flower garden with an arbor and cupid fountain, but actually staring into streaming streaks of golden sunlight that turned dust motes into swirling galaxies.

Anderson, who had been filling March in about the Sharp homicide, was saying, "I spent the morning at that ice rink and this time we've got that evil bitch *cold*."

March turned his attention from the swirling

dust to his former partner, and tried to smile at Anderson's unintentional joke. But March would have needed his entire face to accomplish that, and only half of it was working.

"There were no prints on the skate," Anderson said, pacing, spiffy in shirt and tie and suspenders and no jacket, badge pinned at his waistband, holstered gun tucked inside, "but we expected that."

"Don' geh cawk-ee," March advised his friend.

"I won't get cocky."

"Don' unner-esstuh-may—"

"I won't underestimate her, either. You want me to stop back, later? After I talk to her?"

March shrugged with his good shoulder.

Anderson halted his pacing, his pleasant features contorted into an unpleasant near scowl. "Jesus, Bill—you do care about this, don't you? You are glad she's finally slipped up?"

March stared into a shaft of golden light where dust motes swam.

March's lovely blond wife—who was looking haggard these days but almost always wore a smile on Anderson's not infrequent visits—stepped onto the sunporch in a white sundress with a pitcher of sun tea. She might have been a nurse, just as this white screened-in porch with its white wrought-iron–and-glass furnishings might have been a hospital room.

"You shouldn't have," Anderson told her as she poured the tea into waiting glasses. "I can't stay today. I'm on duty. . . ."

"Stay for a while," Debbie March said cheerily, but there was desperation in her voice.

In her late forties, Debbie had married a vital, robust man's man and now a few short years later found herself bound to an invalid. She had met her second husband, Bill March, after her first husband was murdered by a disgruntled ex–business associate; March had brought the murderer to justice and along the way won the widow, who had urged him to leave the department and become a man of leisure. She finally had her wish.

Anderson made it a point to see March at least once a week, and usually it was two or three times, evenings, or on Anderson's days off. They would sit and watch ESPN together in the home's media room, and occasionally Anderson would bring a John Wayne videotape; they were both fans, particularly of the actor's westerns. They had watched *The Searchers* together half a dozen times, *Rio Bravo* almost that many. Now and then they sat out on this sunporch, and sometimes Anderson brought March up to date on department matters.

March didn't say much. Anderson didn't know whether it was because speaking was so difficult, or because the former detective was embarrassed to speak in such a slurred, halting fashion, which inevitably, awkwardly, led to drooling. His spirits were, not surprisingly, up and down; mostly down.

Privately, Debbie had told Anderson that the

doctors expressed little hope for improvement.

So Anderson sat and sipped a glass of sun tea while Debbie joined them on the sunporch with small talk about family and friends. Anderson did not mention Mrs. Sterling again, and March did not join in the conversation, merely continuing to study the dust motes dancing in the shafts of sunlight.

The comfortably homey exterior of Wesley House, with its stained-oak slatted siding and lushly wooded surroundings, looked more like a big, sprawling house than an institution designed to process society's problem children. It was built on a piece of land that sloped away from the street, and Anderson tooled his unmarked car around the massive building into the well-shaded parking lot at the rear, where another floor revealed itself, a receiving area.

The detective was pleased to see Mrs. Sterling's red Sunbird parked in the lot. Feeling smug, he headed toward the building, past several benches that added to the Wesley grounds' park-like setting; on one of the benches, a skinny male former cocaine dealer Anderson had busted several years ago, who was sitting reading a Stephen King novel, paled and turned away as the detective passed.

But Anderson's smugness quickly faded. Soon he found himself questioning a self-composed, calmly patronizing woman who seemed to view him as a mere mild annoyance.

"So you had *nothing* to do with this," Anderson said.

Mrs. Sterling, seated primly on the brown nubby couch, quietly lovely in a pale blue long-sleeve blouse with her gold cross finding a resting place between her breasts, her hands folded in the lap of her flowing light blue floral-print dress, replied, "Why would I harm a person I barely knew?"

"Well," Anderson smirked, "when it comes to shopping for murder, you are something of an impulse buyer."

Almost absently, her eyes not on him, she said, "I hope this won't impede Jessica Ann's progress with her skating." Now she glanced up at him. "She has a competition coming up, you know."

Anderson, pacing between questions, loomed over her; his thought had been to give her a sense of being cornered, but though she was seated on that couch, pinned against the wall, it was as if he were the trapped one.

"You were seen talking to Jessica Ann."

She shrugged, barely, her soft-focus blond beauty framed by the daisies of a quaint comforter draped over the couch. "I was there in the afternoon," she said matter-of-factly. "Just watching."

He couldn't keep his exasperation out of his voice. "I have witness statements, Mrs. Sterling."

Patiently, as if explaining to a child, she looked up at him and said, "I merely told Jessica Ann that we shouldn't talk. That the court didn't want us to have contact."

"But you *did* have contact!"

The china-blue eyes widened. "We were separated by an inch of Plexiglas, Sergeant."

"This is going to have to be reported to the court."

"Don't all murders have to be reported to the court?" she asked innocently.

He bit off the words: "I'm talking about you seeing your daughter."

With dignified indignation, she said, "Sergeant—a man is *dead* . . . and you're concerned about keeping a mother from her daughter?" She frowned, shook her head, incredulous. "Where are your values?"

He leaned in, teeth clenched. "And where were you at the time of the murder?"

"Right here in my room," she said, gesturing to the cement walls and shabby furnishings around her. "You are aware we have to sign in and out?"

"I'm aware that security at a day care center is tighter. It wouldn't take David Copperfield to sneak in and out of this place."

"Well, I didn't. Besides, there are people here who feel about me much the same way you do."

He frowned at her. "What's that supposed to mean?"

Her smile pretended to be sweet, but he could see the acid in it as she said, "It means that if I strayed from the straight and narrow path, some of my 'friends' here at Wesley House would be sure to let you know. What is the expression? They'd 'drop a dime'?"

He laughed, once. "Did you learn that one at Oakdale?"

"Actually, yes. On some television show. We had cable, you know."

What a piece of work this woman was.

Then he said, "I'm the one who had to inform the wife, Matthew Sharp's wife."

Her tongue and teeth produced a *tsk*. "How awful for you."

"Seems she's Russian, skater herself. Sharp met her when they were both with the Disney ice show. All alone now . . . except for the child."

"Child?"

"She's expecting. Sharp would've been a father."

"Tragic."

He paced again, then planted himself before her and dropped a bomb he'd been saving: "Your car was seen in the Sports Center parking lot."

Another shrug. "I never denied being there."

"It was seen after you say you left. It was the only car in the lot, after hours. . . ."

"*My* car?"

He nodded. "A red Sunbird."

"With my license number?"

"The, uh, witness didn't get a license number. But it was a red Sunbird."

Very innocently, she asked, "Do I have the only red Sunbird in the area, Sergeant?"

He ignored that. "You had a confrontation with Matthew Sharp in full view of witnesses. You screamed at him!"

"Haven't you heard, Sergeant?" she asked, and she lightly tapped her left forearm. "I have an implant that makes me behave."

"Implant," he said, and paced some more.

Then he fixed himself in front of her again and bared his teeth in a terrible smile. "You know what *I* think?"

"I'm sure I couldn't imagine."

"I think you implanted that hockey skate in Matthew Sharp's back thirty-seven times," he said, each word like a blow of the skate. "And I think maybe what you need is a thirty-eight caliber implant. . . . *That* is what I think."

She gazed up at him with what seemed like pained concern, genuine compassion. "How *is* Lieutenant March?"

Anderson's mouth tightened. His voice was very soft as he uttered, "He's a damn vegetable. Half paralyzed. Half the time he keeps company with a drool cup. Happy?"

"Pity," she said, shaking her head, her expression a convincing approximation of sincere sympathy. "Such a lovely man. . . ."

Then coldness iced her voice over and she reached for the magazine she'd been reading (*Martha Stewart's Living*) and added, "Close the door on your way out, would you, Sergeant? . . . I treasure what little privacy I have in this place."

He looked down at her, sitting there beneath

the placid oil painting of the Old Mill, her eyes on her magazine, clearly letting him know the interview was over, and she did not look back up at him when he said, "Sure," and left her there, and shut the door behind him.

Chapter Fourteen

At the far end of the living room of the Conway home, by glass doors leading out onto the deck, Jessica Ann—hair ponytailed back, pretty as the May afternoon in her plaid jumper, which she'd worn to school—sat working on a jigsaw puzzle, blessedly lost in it. The girl enjoyed the peacefulness of a room that, despite its name, nobody in this house did much living in.

Her aunt had decorated the home, and the living room was dominated by Queen Anne furnishings—all cherry wood and curved lines and needlepoint. This house was every bit as nice as where she'd lived before, the Sterling house in Woodcreek—maybe nicer; but the brocade wallpaper and deep green upholstery and the antique knickknacks made it very different. Above the spinet piano, just behind Jessica Ann as she worked at the 700-piece puzzle that her Uncle Paul had given her, was a sampler that said, "Down by the Old Mill Stream," and the walls were rife with Wyeth prints and floral watercolors and idyllic Currier & Ives–style landscapes. The Sterling house, decorated by Mommy, had been a knickknack-free zone, and each stark white wall bore a single, simply and elegantly framed print whose colors were coordinated with the roses and turquoise of the drapes and the tasteful yet functional furnishings.

Several other rooms in the Conway house—the dining area off the kitchen, and the master bedroom—were Early American in style, and Aunt Beth seemed to have worked hard at creating a warmth of atmosphere lacking in the Sterling house. Jessica Ann liked it here okay, but thought the place was a little cluttered, and that Aunt Beth was trying too hard.

The picture in front of her was two-thirds complete and depicted a loon flying low over a lake against the backdrop of a sprawling gothic lodge, a resort called Mohunk Mountain House somewhere in New York that Uncle Paul had given a seminar at once. But there were many more pieces to assemble before the picture would be complete.

She hadn't heard Aunt Beth enter. Jessica Ann first sensed her aunt's presence when Beth settled herself on the piano bench, just behind the girl, who smiled back pleasantly at her aunt, whose solemn expression didn't necessarily signal anything special. After all, Aunt Beth had been depressed ever since Mommy got out of prison.

"Jessy," Aunt Beth said, "we need to talk."

"Oh," Jessica Ann said, fitting another piece into the puzzle, making the loon more distinct.

"I'm . . . I'm afraid I have some very troubling news, dear."

After what she'd been through these last several years, Jessica Ann did not take such words lightly; she almost spun toward her aunt as she asked, "What is it?"

Aunt Beth sighed, trying to find the words; in her sleeveless cotton top and little blue skirt, she seemed more a child than Jessica Ann.

"Your skating instructor," she began haltingly, "last night . . ."

Jessica Ann demanded, *"What?"*

Aunt Beth wasn't looking at her. The concern on her face was mingled with something else, something odd—smugness?

"Sergeant Anderson was here a little while ago," Aunt Beth said, gazing past the girl at the puzzle, "and he wanted to talk to you, but I put him off."

"What? Why?" Frustration and rage rose in the girl. "I'm not a baby!"

"I know, I know." And Aunt Beth seemed to be looking at Jessica Ann with true, pure concern now. "But you've been through so much. . . ."

An alarm inside the child went off, and the

words tumbled out: "Is Mommy all right?"

Aunt Beth smirked and, of all things, laughed. "Oh, she's all right, all right . . . physically."

The confrontation between Mommy and her skating instructor flashed through the child's brain, speeded up, but with an awful clarity.

The girl asked, "Did something happen to Matt?"

Aunt Beth sighed again, nodded.

"An accident?"

"Not an accident."

"Well, what then . . . ?"

". . . Murder."

An all too familiar word in this family.

And even as the thought of Matt dead, Matt murdered, careened through her brain, even as the girl tried to make that concept real, let alone make sense of it, Jessica Ann knew her aunt was behaving weirdly. She could sense, under all that concern—and Aunt Beth was concerned, Jessica Ann did not doubt that—was self-satisfaction.

Underneath it was, *I told you so*.

Someone was saying, "No, no, oh no, oh no . . ." over and over again; finally Jessica Ann realized it was herself.

Her aunt took the weeping, trembling child in her arms and guided her from the table to the nearby couch, a beautiful Queen Anne piece of cherry wood and rich green upholstery only slightly less comfortable than the back of a pickup truck. Beth sat with the girl, holding her tenderly.

"I'm sorry, Jessy," she said, "so sorry. . . ."

Finally the girl managed, "What happened?"

Aunt Beth shook her head, no. "It's too horrible. . . ."

But Jessica Ann insisted. *"What happened?"*

Aunt Beth swallowed and said, "Multiple stab wounds . . . with a skate."

The odd formality of that must have been how Sergeant Anderson had put it: *Multiple stab wounds with a skate.* The girl tried to make sense of that, but couldn't, could only shake her head at the horror of it.

Finally she looked at her aunt, whose pretty features had frozen into a solemn mask, in that cold, inappropriate way Mommy had sometimes, not reacting like a normal person would to a tragedy, with tears, confusion, rage.

A different kind of horror, a quiet kind, was in Jessica Ann's voice as she said to her aunt, "You think Mommy did it."

Aunt Beth, eyes flashing, defensive and also accusatory, asked, "You spoke to her yesterday, didn't you? At the skating rink?"

"Yes," the girl admitted. "She was there watching. I wasn't going to pretend she didn't exist."

Aunt Beth pressed on, righteously. "And your skating instructor had words with your mother?"

"Not really," Jessica Ann shrugged. "Just told Mommy not to come around, 'cause of the court order."

Aunt Beth was shaking her head. "Jessy, there are witnesses . . ."

That startled the girl. "To the murder?"

"No! No . . . to you two talking." She tossed her head and her shoulder-length brown hair shimmered. "To your mother *screaming* at your skating instructor."

Jessica Ann, swallowing back tears, was shaking her head, no. "She didn't do this."

"How can you be so certain?"

She shrugged. "Just am."

Aunt Beth withdrew her arm from around the girl, and straightened herself as she sat, chin up, saying, "Your mother is probably going to be back in prison very soon, but in the meantime, under no circumstances are you to have any contact with her."

"But Aunt Beth—"

Her aunt sprang to her feet, then leaned in to the girl as she said, "If she walks up to you, walk away. Do you understand? Walk away!"

And Aunt Beth walked away.

Jessica Ann rose from the couch and stumbled over to the table, where she began working on the puzzle again, in something like slow motion; it was as if the girl were in a trance.

A few pieces later, the loon had become clear.

And she fell upon the puzzle, covering her head with her locked hands, trying to seal out the world as she wept for Matt, and for her mother, who she knew would be blamed.

Chapter Fifteen

Seated before Dr. Price's desk like a naughty child called to the principal's office, Mrs. Sterling—in a frilly white blouse and a black, gaily floral jumper, the ever-present gold cross dangling between her breasts—was adjusting her sleeve, rebuttoning the cuff.

Price had just examined her left forearm and found the incision healed, the swelling down, the redness gone. He was settling himself behind his desk, with that casual yet professional look he had perfected: blue shirt with a yellow and green golfing-print tie, tan slacks, Hush Puppies. Mozart by Muzak was filtering lightly in. Mrs. Sterling, with her dazed, absent expression, didn't seem to be paying any attention to either Price or Mozart.

"I'm taking you off the anti-inflammatory and the painkiller," he said.

Still seated sideways from his inspection of her arm, she turned her head slowly toward him, the head of a robot pivoting, and met his eyes with china blues that seemed bright despite the dullness of her expression. "Will that make me feel . . . better?"

"How so?"

"Not so . . . sluggish. Lethargic. I feel like I'm sleepwalking sometimes."

He raised an eyebrow, cocked his head sympathetically. "I'm afraid that's a side effect of your antipsychotic medication."

"The implant."

He nodded. "The implant . . . though as your system acclimates itself to this, shall we say, friendly intrusion, you should feel something of your old buoyancy return."

A tiny smile formed. "I felt something of my old 'buoyancy' yesterday."

Was she raising the subject for him, so he didn't have to? The murder at the Ferndale Sports Center?

Innocently, he asked, "You did?"

"Yes." Her mouth tightened, not a smile, not a frown, either; her hands were folded contritely in her lap. "When I argued with Jessica Ann's skating instructor."

Price nodded somberly. "Who was murdered."

She looked pointedly at him. "Not by me."

"I didn't accuse you of that."

148

"No." She swallowed. She turned her gaze to the window, its blinds shut, its view of the parking lot obscured. "No, you didn't, Doctor. . . ." And now she looked at him; so pretty, prettier than ever with this new, girlish femininity. "John—thank you for that."

"For what?"

"Not accusing me."

"I don't believe you did it."

"You don't?"

"No." He came around the desk, pulled a chair up, and sat backwards on it, facing her. "Do you want to talk about it? Let's start with the argument."

She told him, concluding with, "For a moment, the old feeling . . . the old rage . . . it was there."

Like a dormant volcano, he thought, *still occasionally capable of bubbling, even of spewing lava*.

"I told you," he said, "that you're still yourself . . . you have the same feelings, even the same impulses . . . you just don't act upon them as . . . indiscriminately."

She reached out as if to touch his hand, then pulled back, apparently thinking better of it. "John . . . there's something I have to ask you. It . . . it relates to my fears about this medication."

He leaned forward. "What is it?" He had to work to suppress *darling*.

Her head was lowered, her eyes hooded. "It makes me so tired, and when I go to sleep . . . even if it's only a nap, in the afternoon . . . I go *deep* asleep. A dreamless sleep . . ."

"That's unlikely."

"John, it's like a coma. I awake feeling drugged, then once I've been up and around, I feel almost refreshed. Not so sluggish."

"Is this after your first cup of coffee?" he smiled.

"John, please . . . this is serious."

"I know. But even without coffee, what you describe is normal enough with medication this strong."

She shook her head and sighed. "John . . . last night . . . I was asleep during the time that Jessica Ann's instructor . . . what was his name?"

Price shrugged again. "Mark something?"

"No—I think it's Matt something. Anyway, when her instructor was killed, I was asleep in my room at Wesley House. At least . . . I think I was."

He began to understand her. "You mean, you're wondering if you might have been . . ."

"Not sleepwalking. More like, what?"

"A blackout?"

She nodded forcefully, as she said, "Yes. Yes. Could I have done this, and not know it? Could I have killed him, and not remember?"

"There's nothing in the research that indicates this medication has any such side effect," he assured her, but he also knew that Mrs. Sterling was the first true field test of the powerful antipsychotic drug. And it would take a powerful psychotic like Mrs. Sterling to truly test it.

"Sergeant Anderson said a car like mine was

seen in the parking lot," she said, "just before the killing."

He frowned. "That little red rental Ekhardt arranged?"

"Yes."

"That's a pretty common vehicle."

"I know." She was touching the cross at her neck, fiddling with it absently. "But it's a . . . troubling coincidence."

"Do you think you might have done this?"

"I don't know. I don't think so."

"Were you mad enough to kill him?"

"Of course not!" She continued to stroke the gold cross at her neck. "Without this medication, I might have slapped him."

"He wasn't slapped. He was slashed and stabbed with an ice skate."

She shrugged, let go of the cross, and for a moment the old coldness was back in her voice as she said, "That seems inefficient."

This comment chilled him, but he pressed on, saying, "Have you said anything of this to Anderson?"

"No! Just that I was sleeping in my room when it happened. Nothing of my fears about . . . blackouts or whatever."

"Good. Might I suggest you keep Neal Ekhardt informed?"

She nodded numbly. "I suppose with the police coming around, I should be talking to my attorney."

"No question. In the meantime, I'll have a talk with Sergeant Anderson myself."

Her eyes flashed, nostrils flared. "You're not going to tell him about—"

"No! Of course not. Your concerns, your fears, are your business—and mine, as your doctor. But I've known Max Anderson a long time, and maybe I can convince him he's on the wrong track."

Now she did touch him, reaching out and squeezing his hand.

But that was as far as it went, and she was soon gone, and within the hour, he'd gotten word to Anderson, who came right over and settled into the same chair as Mrs. Sterling, opposite Price's desk.

"Sergeant," Price said, "it's a physiological impossibility that Mrs. Sterling could have committed this crime with the antipsychotic implant in place."

Anderson had come in wearing a smirk; the smirk deepened as he asked, "How do you know it's in place?"

"I saw her this afternoon." Price gestured to his own left forearm. "This is a silicon rod underneath the skin, replaced surgically, on a semi-annual basis—it doesn't come with a zipper."

"Oh, that's cute," Anderson said, then he leaned forward menacingly. "Did you ever consider, Doctor, that maybe this isn't a matter of science or medicine . . . that maybe little Mommy doesn't have a chemical deficiency in her brain, but a blackness in her heart?"

Anderson's archness amused Price, who batted the air at the ridiculousness of that, saying, "You're looking for a vampire to drive a stake through, Sergeant." Then the psychiatrist leaned forward and said, quite seriously, "This is a woman with an *illness*."

"I know the cure," Anderson smirked, patting the automatic in his waistband-tucked holster.

Price could only shake his head and smile sadly at this macho bullshit. "Yeah, well you make a fine frontier marshal, Max," he said. "Just not much of a detective."

That got the cop's attention, and he straightened in his chair. "What are you talkin' about?"

"The viciousness of this killing doesn't *begin* to fit Mrs. Sterling's psychological profile."

"Psychological profile my ass! John, she commits two kinds of murders—her calculated, black-widow style send-offs for her wealthy husbands . . ."

"Unproven. Sheer speculation."

". . . and spur-of-the-moment murders of people who stand between her and what she wants."

Price laughed. "And that skating instructor stood between her and her precious daughter, I suppose?"

Anderson, arms folded, leaning back cockily in the chair, nodded and said, "Bingo."

The psychiatrist sighed, and sat forward, trying one more time to reason with his old high school buddy. "What you fail to understand, Sergeant, is that Mrs. Sterling is *not* sadistic . . . she takes no pleasure in killing. She merely . . . removes obstacles—as cleanly as possible."

"Cleanly! That skating instructor was stabbed thirty-seven times!"

"Thank you for making my point, Max. Anyway, it doesn't take Freud to figure you out. I know what this is really about."

"Oh you do, Doctor? What's your diagnosis, then?"

Price shrugged. "You blame Mrs. Sterling for your partner's misfortune."

"Wait just one minute!" Anderson erupted, jumping to his feet, almost crawling over the desk. "Bill March had a stroke when that bitch broke jail!"

"And did 'that bitch' force-feed March those four packs of cigarettes a day for forty years? Or are you more interested in putting 'Mommy' away than finding out who's really responsible for this killing?"

The words sat Anderson back down again. His tight, defensive expression melted into a blank, putty-like mass, willing to be molded by reason.

Price had, to some degree anyway, gotten through to him.

"You think?" Anderson asked.

Price nodded, and took the detective through it again slowly, chapter and verse, on how Mrs. Sterling could not possibly be the murderer.

But Price left out the possibility of blackouts; the field research on that subject was not complete.

Chapter Sixteen

Central Middle School—a three-story, vaguely deco tan-brick building built as a high school in 1937—lay peacefully on green, manicured grounds in the midst of a residential section, not far from the Ferndale Public Safety Building and nearby Cedar Street, a fairly busy thoroughfare.

In this quiet setting, Central—when school was in session—was like a slumbering beast within whom microorganisms were busily, and fairly quietly, going about their business. During classes the brick-walled hallways were largely deserted; a bulletin board decorated with pastel paper flowers waited to remind the students that Mother's Day was coming, an award case near the forensics room displayed debate and speech trophies, posters announced the spring dance, a

155

track meet this Saturday, and that nominations were due in the office for the Thelma Withers Excellence in Education award.

But, as in almost any school, when the bell rang announcing the end of class, all hell broke loose.

As kids streamed out of Language Arts, Jessica Ann Sterling—in white tennies, red socks, blue denim cuffed shorts, and a white top adorned with red hearts, a navy blue bookpack on her back—was lagging behind. Lucy Peters fell in step with her.

Lucy—a slender, pretty brunette, taller than Jessica Ann, in a blue-and-white striped top and denim shorts, also with a bookpack on her back—was watching Jessica Ann with concern.

This was not lost on Jessica Ann, who liked Lucy well enough—they were in chorus together—but didn't appreciate this attention. Jessica Ann kept mostly to herself; she did not have a best friend, and—as one of the top students in school—engendered a certain amount of resentment from her classmates. Added to this was the common knowledge of who Jessica Ann's mother was.

"You okay?" Lucy asked as they walked slowly along.

"Sure," Jessica Ann said.

"Are you ready for the history test?"

"I guess."

They walked some more. To Lucy, the silence was awkward; to Jessica Ann, blessed.

Then Lucy blurted, "You shouldn't pay any attention to what kids say."

Jessica Ann glared at her companion. "Who says I pay any attention?"

"Nobody," Lucy said defensively. "I just thought at lunch you mighta heard . . ."

"What?" Jessica Ann asked sharply, knowing exactly what Lucy meant. Jessica Ann knew what the kids were whispering about, some laughing, some horrified, stealing looks at her, pointing; the murder of Matt Sharp was splashed all over the TV and papers.

"Just don't pay any attention to them, that's all," Lucy said.

"Whatever," Jessica Ann said, and her mother popped out right in front of them.

"Jessica Ann!" Mommy cried out, as if warning her of an oncoming car.

It seemed like Mommy had materialized, not just stepped out from around a corner where she'd been waiting, almost hiding. Lucy sucked in air, took a step back, and then scurried forward like a frightened mouse down into the nearby stairwell.

Jessica Ann stood petrified as her mother—looking almost silly in little-girl attire: a puffy-sleeved frilly blouse under a floral jumper—approached her with a pitiful expression, hands clasped before her like a beggar.

"I'm sorry, honey," Mommy said contritely. "I didn't mean to startle you."

"You shouldn't be here!"

157

"I had to *see* you. . . ."

The hallway was almost empty, most of the kids well on their way to class. Jessica Ann, alarmed by her mother's presence, gathered the petite woman and walked her toward the nearest corner, where a bulletin board trumpeting OUTSTANDING STUDENT OF THE WEEK (Eduardo Melindez) met the double doors of the library.

"I'm not supposed to see you," Jessica Ann insisted, looking side to side, relieved no kids or teachers were around. "You're gonna go back to jail if—"

"That's why we have to talk," Mommy said with a desperate urgency. She looked very pretty, but also very sad; her eyes were moist, red.

Daughter scolded mother, "We're not *supposed* to talk. . . ."

"Your skating instructor, that awful accident . . ."

"It wasn't an accident," Jessica Ann said firmly. "You don't accidentally get stabbed a hundred times."

Mommy leaned forward, her expression so seized with emotion that it took Jessica Ann aback; she'd never seen Mommy like this.

"I didn't do it," Mommy said, touching her heart. "You have to believe me!"

"I do."

Now it was Mommy who seemed taken aback.

"You . . . you do?" Hope sprang into Mommy's eyes; she was almost smiling. Her fingers touched the gold cross at her throat. "Do . . . do you really?"

"You'da stabbed him once."

Mommy gasped.

The girl shrugged. "Or maybe choked him."

"Oh God!" Mommy cried, and covered her mouth with trembling hands; tears were welling. "You hate me, don't you?"

And now the emotion welled within Jessica Ann as she reached out and touched her mother's arm. "No, no, I don't hate you," the girl said, and now she was the one pleading to be believed.

"Jessica Ann!"

Both mother and daughter whirled toward the sound of the voice, emanating from the very nearby open door where, from within the library, Mrs. Jensen—former assistant principal at the McKinley School, currently head librarian at Central Middle School—leaned out with a stern expression.

"Where's your next class?" the teacher demanded curtly. She was a usually pleasant looking woman in her early forties, but her expression right now was anything but pleasant.

"F-first floor, west wing," Jessica Ann managed.

"Then you'd better get a move on." The teacher eyed the girl's mother, who had withdrawn into the corner like a child being punished. "You're Mrs. Sterling, aren't you? You're not supposed to be seeing your daughter—"

Jessica Ann touched the teacher's arm lightly;

the girl's head was back and her eyes narrow as she cautioned, "I wouldn't do that if I were you. . . ."

Mommy gasped again, and—clearly embarrassed, perhaps weeping—pushed wordlessly past the teacher, into the library, where an exit awaited.

Now the teacher moved into the corner, bewildered by this exchange, as a trio of straggling boys came out of the library, glancing behind them at the blond woman who had just rushed past; the boys had recognized the notorious Mrs. Sterling, of course, and were murmuring in contemplation of that. Jessica Ann, feeling shell-shocked, had gathered her composure and was heading toward the stairwell, over which a banner said, THANK YOU PARENTS . . . YOUR SUPPORT IS APPRECIATED! TO ALL OUR TEACHERS . . . THANKS FOR A JOB WELL DONE!

"So . . ." a taunting male voice behind her on the stairs called out to her, ". . . that's your old lady, huh?"

She glanced behind her disgustedly. It was Nate Allen, a big baby-faced kid with glasses and dark hair in a Moe of the Three Stooges haircut and a bad, bullying attitude to match; she'd had trouble with him since McKinley.

He was right on her heels, gleefully saying, "What'd they do, let her out of the nuthouse for the afternoon?"

His two pals behind him were giggling and jostling each other.

"Must be pretty cool," the boy said, as they neared the bottom of the stairs, "havin' a serial mom!"

They were on the landing now, and Jessica Ann whirled on the kid and, with a fury and strength that surprised even her, she grabbed onto his Beavis and Butt-head T-shirt and slammed him into the brick wall, making his bangs fly up like his hair had exploded.

"Maybe it runs in the family," she snarled up at him, her tiny fists clutching the T-shirt; he was looking down at her with wide eyes and his mouth dropped open. "Maybe I'll kill *you*—in your *sleep*!"

And she shoved him again, letting go of him, not afraid of anything he might do or say.

But before the shocked boy or his two amazed friends—frozen on the stairs above them—could do or say anything else, an adult voice called down to them, "Jessica Ann!"

A man's voice.

And Nate Allen and his two stooges scrambled like rats across the landing and down the final half flight of stairs to the first floor.

Seeing who it was coming down—Sergeant Anderson, the police detective, in a denim shirt and suspenders and jeans, unwrapping a stick of gum as he casually walked down the steps—Jessica Ann started to follow the boys; but Anderson's voice halted her: "Wait a minute, wait a minute, I want to talk to you for a second."

And by the time he had finished saying all that,

161

he was on the landing facing her. He was chuckling, popping the gum into his mouth, saying, "Hey, you really got in that kid's face. Gum?"

"No," Jessica Ann said sullenly. "My mother didn't get my teeth straightened so I could ruin them."

"No," he grinned, "I guess you don't wanna chew gum, not with braces."

She smiled at him and nodded but it wasn't a real smile. Did he honestly think she was fooled by this nice act?

"You remember me, don't you, Jessica Ann?"

Without looking at him, she said coldly, "You work with Lieutenant March."

"Yeah, well, I did," he said, folding his arms, leaning against the brick wall. "Till he got sick. . . . After what your mother did."

She turned on him, glaring. "I'm sorry he got sick, but my mother had nothing to do with it." She moved past him, saying, "Excuse me—I'm going to be late for class. . . ."

He blocked her path, and they did a little ballet in the small area, as he maneuvered her around. "Now, I just wanna talk to you, just wanna talk to you for a few seconds. . . ."

And then she was standing with her back to the wall as he barred the way.

He asked, "You talk to your mother lately?"

She laughed at him. "You mean you didn't see us just now?" Then she openly mocked him, tickling the air with her fingers: "Aren't you following us around, hiding behind bushes and stuff?"

Like one kid caught by another, he laughed and said, "Matter of fact, I am. . . . Talked to her yesterday, too, didn't you?"

"You know I did," the girl said indignantly. Then more quietly, cooperatively, she continued, "At the skating rink. And Mommy and my instructor did get in a little tiff—but nothing Mommy would kill over."

He leaned in; his voice was kind. "You sure about that, Jessica Ann?"

"Well," Jessica Ann said, frowning thoughtfully, as if troubled, looking up at him with her mother's big blue eyes, "I'm sure of one thing."

"Yeah, what's that?"

"They oughta stick one of those things in *your* arm," she scowled. "*You're* the nut."

And as the startled detective reared back, she slipped by him and hustled down the stairs and was inside the classroom where a history test awaited, just as the final bell sounded.

The detective, on the landing, was shaking his head and chuckling, saying to himself, "Smart kid . . . smart kid."

And, having learned a lesson, Sergeant Max Anderson left Central Middle School.

Chapter Seventeen

Smoking her third Salem cigarette since arriving, Mrs. Sterling paced in the greenroom of KWQC-TV in Naperville, Illinois, a suburb of Chicago. The greenroom was a small gray cubicle about the color of her cigarette smoke, and—as she was attired in an elegantly conservative gray suit patterned with tiny white crosses that made the jacket and dress beneath seem a lighter gray—Mrs. Sterling almost vanished against the walls, with only her perfectly coiffed blond hair and pale, finely chiseled features to give her away. Her makeup was heavier than usual, as right after she was led to the greenroom, a young woman who announced herself as a makeup artist had cornered her in here with a kit like a shoeshine box, to spruce her up for the TV cameras.

She had driven here, alone, in her red Sunbird; both Dr. Price and Neal Ekhardt had been against this, and declined to accompany her. She was on her own.

And her stomach was jumping. These kind of nerves she had never suffered before the implant; of course, she had never gone on a nationally syndicated television program before the implant, either.

A pleasant looking young man, thirty perhaps, with reddish brown hair and a boyishly ingratiating smile entered, clipboard in hand; he had an almost collegiate look, wearing a sports shirt with a blue-brick pattern, tan jeans, and brown loafers.

"Mrs. Sterling," he said, beaming at her, extending his free hand. "We spoke on the phone— Jerry Karmen. Producer of *The Jenny Rivers Show*."

"Oh! Mr. Karmen." They shook hands; she found his touch as cool as a polished stone. "Pleasure meeting you in person."

"We're grateful to you for coming." He touched her shoulder, smiled a winning half smile. "I'm sure you've had plenty of opportunities . . ."

"And I've said no to them all," she said. "You were the only venue that was willing to meet my terms."

"They were reasonable terms," he shrugged, and he took her gently by the arm and guided her out of the greenroom into the wide corridor, toward the studio.

"I've never done anything like this before," she admitted with a nervous laugh, as he ushered her along, hand at the crook of her arm.

"Nothing to worry about. Just follow Jenny's lead. You'll like her—she treats her guests like family."

He pushed through the double doors into Studio A and the vast, high-ceilinged, brightly lighted chamber was like some bizarre modern church. The producer steered her safely over the cords and cables that snaked underfoot, past massive cameras operated by surprisingly slovenly attired, bored looking camera operators.

"Thank you for giving me an opportunity to tell my side," she said.

"You've been getting a raw deal in the media," Karmen said with a little shrug. "We're here to balance that out."

They were moving past the studio audience, who sat in folding chairs on risers; funny how cheap this all looked in person. Cheapest of all was the rabble sitting there, awful creatures in clothing Sears wouldn't sell, leaning forward google-eyed, gargoyles gawking at her, murmuring like a gathering insect swarm.

"And I won't have to answer any questions from . . ." She nodded toward the gaping spectators. ". . . *them*."

"No, no," Karmen said, almost laughing. Then he leaned in reassuringly and said, "This is just a simple one-on-one interview with Jenny. She's on your side. We're *all* on your side."

"No surprises," Mrs. Sterling reminded him, with a strained smile.

The producer was escorting her in a gentlemanly manner; up ahead was the elaborate pink neon–trimmed set, a blue armchair where Jenny Rivers sat, the makeup artist touching her up, and, waiting for Mrs. Sterling, a comfy-looking floral couch, all set against the soothing pink and blue pastels of the painted backdrop.

"The only surprise," Karmen said, "is how good it's going to feel to be vindicated. . . . Mrs. Sterling, I'd like you to meet our star, Jenny Rivers."

And the lovely blond hostess—impeccable in a dark navy pantsuit, her perfect features so thick with makeup it was as if the luminous brown eyes were staring out from within a flawless mask—shook Mrs. Sterling's hand, saying, "So nice to have you here, please have a seat," as the courtly Karmen deposited her on the floral couch and a scruffy technician moved in to run the cord of a small lapel microphone up under the jacket of her gray suit.

She couldn't really see the audience of lowlifes any longer—the lights above and spotted around and about created a white blur punctuated with crosses of glare that made everything but the little world of the set indistinguishable—but she could hear them out there, mumbling, rumbling, like an engine on a plane about to go out.

Jenny and Karmen were huddled over his clipboard, going over things; Mrs. Sterling couldn't hear what they were saying, and she glanced about the set, noting how artificial and thread-bare it all seemed, in contrast to the apparent perfection that came across over the air.

Soon a floor director was counting down, and then the announcer's voice, small and unampli-fied in the studio, called out, "It's *The Jenny Rivers Show*, where *your* opinions count—and here's the first lady of daytime talk—*Jenneeee Rivers!*"

Applause and cheers rang through the studio, then settled down (at the off-camera announcer's direction), as Jenny Rivers turned to the nearest camera and said to it as if to a close friend, "Thank you, Brad . . . thank you, studio audi-ence. We do have a remarkable guest today, and I still don't know how my producer pulled this one off . . . but sitting right next to me is . . . for-give me . . ."

And these last two words were directed at Mrs. Sterling, who smiled sweetly, as Jenny Rivers turned her oh-so-compassionate gaze upon her guest, even as, in the control booth, the director of the switched feed centered on a two-shot of the women, to catch Mrs. Sterling's inevitable upcoming change of expression.

". . . the 'Killer Mommy' you've heard so much about. . . ."

She felt as though she'd been struck a blow in her stomach; this was not the introduction she'd expected, and warning bells began to sound in her mind. She was in trouble. She was in trouble, here. . . .

Jenny Rivers, hands folded primly, was leaning forward with concern, her voice warm as she said, "It must be painful, being characterized by such a painful phrase," as if she hadn't been the one who'd uttered it. "Mrs. Sterling, what is it like to be at the center of such a media storm?"

She drew a breath, hopeful that—the tastelessly cruel introduction past—they would settle into a meaningful interview. Unaware that the control-booth director had superimposed across her image, toward the bottom of the screen, her name and the words *Convicted Murderer*, Mrs. Sterling said with quiet dignity, "I'm living a quiet life. I'm in a halfway house."

"I understand you're in an experimental program. Some kind of new medication . . . ?"

"Yes."

Jenny Rivers was beginning to know that she was in trouble, too; Mrs. Sterling may have been a notorious public figure, but she was not a seasoned talk show guest. A simple *yes* or *no* was not the answer to any question on a talk show.

"I don't know if you're free to speak about this," the hostess pressed on, "I don't know what your attorney has advised you . . ."

Mrs. Sterling laughed once, nervously. "He advised me not to appear."

Jenny Rivers leaned in with the artificial concern that had made her a wealthy young woman, saying gently, "But there's been another murder, and we understand you're again under investigation."

"Yes," Mrs. Sterling said, straightening herself, pleased to finally be getting her day in the court of the public eye, "and that's partly why I'm here. I am absolutely, one hundred percent innocent of that crime."

The audience began to boo, to hiss, to catcall.

This took Mrs. Sterling aback, and Jenny Rivers scolded the crowd with, "Please! Please. . . ." Then she turned to her guest. "Frankly, Mrs. Sterling, it doesn't sound like you're convincing our audience."

"There's really only one person I want to convince," Mrs. Sterling said, and she touched the gold cross at her breast. She turned and looked directly at the camera. "It's a person who's been kept away from me . . . my daughter."

And in Ferndale, in her room in the Conway home, Jessica Ann, watching *The Jenny Rivers Show*, sat on her bed, riveted by her mother's words, and her mother's eyes, which looked directly at her from over the miles, through the television screen. The girl understood the irony of her mother having to drive to Chicago to communicate with her daughter in Ferndale; and she could see in her mother's eyes, hear in her mother's voice, a depth of love that frightened and yet elated her.

But in the studio in Naperville, things were about to take an ugly turn.

Jenny Rivers was saying, "I know our audience

is dying to ask some questions. . . . Brad, do you have our first question?"

It took a moment for that to register, and Mrs. Sterling hadn't yet formed the words of protest when an attractive woman in red, well dressed for this crowd and sharing with Mrs. Sterling a certain country club patina, stepped up to a microphone brandished by Brad out in the audience.

"You say you want your daughter's attention?" the woman asked reasonably. And then the tone turned shrewish: "Is that maybe why you tried to strangle her?"

Feeling as though she were in a bad dream from which she couldn't awake, Mrs. Sterling turned to Jenny Rivers and whispered indignantly, "I was told there wouldn't be any questions from—"

"Mrs. Sterling," Jenny Rivers said without apology, "I don't know who gave you that impression, but if you've seen our show, you know that this is our format. . . ."

And Jenny had turned dismissively away from Mrs. Sterling halfway through that response, her attention on her announcer, signaling him to go ahead with the next question.

Which he did, eliciting the following comment from a young, voluptuous, animated black woman: "You say you love your daughter, right? Well you better get your stuff together before you start layin' your own personal trip on her head, you hear what I'm sayin', girlfriend?"

172

Mrs. Sterling did not respond to this indignity, not directly, not to the foolish questioner, rather turned toward Jenny Rivers, whose demeanor spoke of responsibility and even empathy, saying to the hostess, "I would never hurt my daughter. . . ."

And again Mrs. Sterling looked right into the camera, beseeching anyone out there who might be listening, including God perhaps: "I love my daughter more than life itself. . . ."

Jessica Ann heard; tearful eyes fixed upon the TV positioned high on her bedroom wall, the child clutched her teddy bear, reverting to age six, uttering, "Oh Mommy . . . oh Mommy. . . ."

In the studio audience at *The Jenny Rivers Show*, a weathered-looking, jut-jawed, truck-driverish guy with a barrel chest, beer belly, and John Deere baseball cap was blustering into the microphone provided by Brad: "People like you don't deserve to live! Lethal injection is too damn good for ya! They oughta *hang* your snooty ass. . . ."

"That isn't really a question," Jenny Rivers said daintily, as if to restore a certain sense of decorum before turning to her guest to say, "Mrs. Sterling, you can see the kind of strong feelings you engender in our audience. . . ."

Speaking with tight indignation, quaking with gathering rage, Mrs. Sterling said, "I was promised there would not be any questions from the aud—"

"Let's bring out our second guest," Jenny

Rivers interrupted, swiveling toward the camera. "She has her own strong feelings about this subject—she's been with us before on this show—the sister of one of Mrs. Sterling's alleged victims, *Jolene Jones* . . ."

And onto the set, from where she'd been kept hidden in the wings, strode a smugly smiling Jolene Jones, in a towering wig of tight red curls and a shocking pink minidress that hugged her considerable curves and showed off shapely nyloned legs above black-leather ankle boots with stiletto heels.

"I will not be a part of this," Mrs. Sterling said, stunned, outraged, starting to stand but getting caught by the wire of the lapel mike threaded under her jacket.

Jolene Jones sat next to her on the couch and grasped Mrs. Sterling by the arm and said, "Don't you try to crawl away, you murdering bitch! You're gonna face the fuckin' music, this time!"

In Ferndale, as Jessica Ann watched, horrified for her mother, the obscenities were bleeped out; but they weren't hard to fill in, even for a sheltered child like Jessica Ann.

Mrs. Sterling, face tight with fury, turned away, pulling her arm free, but Jolene leaned in, shouting, "You look at me—*look at me!*"

Her face empty, Mrs. Sterling looked at the woman.

"You killed my sister," Jolene almost whispered. Then her voice rose theatrically: "And someday you're gonna pay for it. You are gonna fuckin' pay!"

"Well," Mrs. Sterling said, straightening prudishly, as if the most offensive thing about this woman was her vile language.

"We'll be right back," Jenny Rivers beamed into the camera, "after a word from our sponsor—Happy Family Dairy."

"Clear," a floor director called, after the cut to commercial.

Jenny Rivers's smiling face dissolved into an angry sneer. "Jerry!" she called.

The boyish producer scurried to her side. "*Yes, Jenny . . .*"

"Did Mrs. Sterling know we were going to take those questions from the audience?" Jenny whispered. "Did she *know* she was going to be appearing with Ms. Jones?"

Mrs. Sterling was on her feet, frantically and furiously fumbling with the cord of the lapel microphone, trying desperately to extricate herself.

The producer's response to his star was superficially respectful but reeked of condescension. "Guests don't get to dictate the terms of their appearance, Jenny."

But the producer had barely got that last word out when Mrs. Sterling, freed from her microphone, was on her feet and looming over him and Jenny.

To the producer, Mrs. Sterling snarled, "You are a liar and a heel!"

But Jolene Jones had risen from the couch behind Mrs. Sterling, replying for producer Karmen: "Yeah, well you're a murdering bitch!"

Barely glancing over her shoulder at the woman, Mrs. Sterling snapped, "Stay away from me."

"Oh, or what?" Jolene sneered. "You gonna fry me, too?"

"It shut your sister up."

Jolene's eyes and nostrils flared and she latched onto Mrs. Sterling's shoulder, pulling her around, saying, "Listen to me, you psycho bitch—"

As casually as picking a daisy, Mrs. Sterling reached up and latched onto that hand on her shoulder and with a simple, powerful twist sent the younger woman to her knees, yowling in pain. The audience watched in shock, completely silent now that the cameras weren't rolling.

Jerry Karmen rose from his subservient position by his star to insert himself between Mrs. Sterling and the now kneeling, weeping Jolene.

"How would you ladies feel about repeating this on camera?" he asked from his crouch, his boyish smile on full wattage.

Then "the Killer Mommy" clutched Karmen by the throat with one forceful hand and hauled him to his feet, his eyes golf-balling with pain and surprise.

"You're lucky I'm mellowed out," she whispered through clenched teeth, then—as if discarding a wrapper—flung the producer into

Jenny Rivers's lap and stormed off the set and out of the studio.

In the control booth, the director said, "Stand by!"

A floor manager called out, "On in three!"

A stunned Jerry Karmen, holding his throat where Mrs. Sterling had clutched it, eyes wide and glazed, sat atop Jenny Jones like a child on his mother's lap.

"We need to talk," she told him with mock sweetness.

Then she disgustedly shoved him off, and he gulped, nodded, and, with clipboard in hand, scurried away like a rat to its hole. A technician was helping the shaken Jolene to the couch.

The cameras were on again, the audience applauding wildly, and Jenny Rivers was gazing into the lens with a dazzling smile worthy of Mrs. Sterling, saying, "Welcome back—and a reminder that on tomorrow's show we'll have Born-Again Full-Body-Tattooed Bikers. . . ."

Chapter Eighteen

Studio B—slightly smaller than the studio where the nationally syndicated *Jenny Rivers Show* was produced—was home to the television station's public affairs shows and other local programming. Cluttered with cables, lights on stands, assorted camera gear, carts with video decks and monitors, as well as set-building materials, Studio B always seemed in a state of flux and even chaos.

At the moment, however, the studio was quiet, a spotlight high in the flies creating a pool of light for Jerry Karmen to pace in. Karmen, ever-present clipboard in hand, was throwing his shadow on a mock brick wall decorated with old movie posters—*Detour*, *Gun Crazy*, *The Girl Hunters*. The producer was waiting for Jenny

Rivers, who had asked him to meet her here for a private talk.

He knew what was coming; he knew what his star's list of complaints would be. And he knew exactly how to counter her charges.

A door opened, throwing a shaft of light as Chris Kline came rushing in, Nicole Miller tie flapping. Chris was currently Jerry's significant other, and the handsome kid—his wetted-back blond hair at odds with his fresh-scrubbed, Arrow-shirt look—was eager to prove himself more than just a pretty face.

"Did you want me, Jerry?" he asked, eyes bright.

"Yeah," Karmen said absently, eyes on the clipboard with its list of upcoming *Jenny Rivers* guests. "See if Phil's got that memo ready—ratings book came in this morning."

"You got it."

Chris had turned to go when Karmen added irritably, "Oh, and can you get rid of some of this garbage?"

Karmen was indicating the brick stage flat with its classic crime movie posters.

"*Film Noir Theater*," Karmen said derisively. "Whose idea was that?"

Chris's face fell, and he nodded and went out, not so much the eager beaver.

Karmen of course knew it was his protégé's idea to put together a late-night program of vintage crime films, hosted by the station's film-buff weatherman, a guy well into his fifties who was due to be put out to pasture. Karmen was really doing his current companion a favor. Chris needed to have some of this film school nonsense drummed out of him. This was television. In this business, having a sense of history meant remembering last month's ratings book.

The click of high heels in the darkness announced his star. She had entered from the other side of Studio B—her office was down that hallway—and emerged into the light a vision of pissed-off blond loveliness.

She planted herself before him, weight evenly distributed on her shapely legs, arms folded tightly across the chest that had required no implants to attract a significant portion of the male daytime demographic. Jenny was one fabulous babe, the best-looking teleprompter reader TV had seen since Mary Hart came out of Cedar Rapids, Iowa.

And she could break your balls at thirty paces.

The lush, overly lipsticked mouth curled into a sneer. "What was the idea today, Jerry?"

"Numbers," he shrugged. "What do you think? I just sent Chris after the latest. You'll see."

"I thought we had an understanding," she said, enunciating each word with newscaster precision. "No more ambushing the guests."

Karmen lifted a hand to his sore neck, where Mrs. Sterling had clutched it. "That woman's not a guest," he said, "she *is* an ambush."

"You got her on the show under false pretenses," Jenny said crisply, big brown eyes flaring. "Never mind the right or wrong of it—word gets around I can't be trusted, we're finished."

"Yeah?"

"Yeah!"

"Yeah? You want to wait for the ratings memo?"

Jenny sighed and regarded him with open distaste. "You are a heel, Jerry—which must come in handy for you, the way you walk all over people."

She shook her head with disgust, blond arcs of hair shimmering, and swiveled away from him, moving back into the darkness, high heels clicking.

From the doorway, framed in light, she paused to say, "I'll be in my office."

"And I'll bring you the numbers."

Then Jenny was gone, and to hell with her, she'd come around when she saw the results, and now Karmen was stuck in Studio B till Chris got back; he paced, peeling back the page on the clipboard, studying the scheduled airdates. He'd had a cancellation by two guests set for the upcoming "Men Having Affairs With Their Mothers-in-Law" show, and needed to reshuffle things to cover.

The sound of high heels, again, in the darkness, caught his attention.

"Jenny?" he called, squinting toward the sound.

Had that been high heels, those few clicks, or just some electrical noise? Or was it merely somebody walking by out in the hallway? He shrugged and returned to his pacing and his scheduling problems.

He did not see, in the darkness, just inside the door Jenny had exited through not so long ago, a blond woman in a severely stylish dark blue dress step gingerly out of her high heels. He did not see the sleekly shapely nyloned legs climbing the wall-mounted steel ladder that led to the catwalk.

He also did not see her up above him, moving along the catwalk among the lighting equipment, though her nyloned feet did cause a squeaking on the steel grating, and he glanced up from his clipboard once, but seeing nothing, shrugged and returned to his scheduling woes.

Up in the flies, the blond woman was shopping; she was looking for just the right item, at just the correct angle. Finding what she needed, she began to unscrew a nut and bolt, and unstring a wound cord.

A *clunk* alerted Karmen, and he glanced up to see the baby spotlight, still plugged in, still shining bright, coming right at him, like the headlight of an oncoming motorcycle. Metal and glass smashed into his forehead, turning off the spotlight, and his lights as well, for a moment anyway.

When he came around, head spinning, pain knifing from temple to temple, he found himself on the studio floor, in a small pool of his own blood—from the gash on his forehead—with

183

shards of glass scattered around him. The metal framework of the spot lay twisted nearby, several of its steel-flap "barn doors" torn loose.

Groggy, groaning, he rolled over on his back. The lights in Studio B were out now, only the red glow of a maintenance blub provided any illumination, and he was trying to summon the energy and will to get to his feet when he heard the single clicks coming toward him.

Woozy, he managed to turn his head and saw the shapely legs walking toward him, one foot in a high heel, the other not, limping toward him, the thud of the nyloned foot followed by the click of the high heel. . . .

When she got to him, hovering over him, he looked up, but he couldn't see her face, only the arcs of shimmering blond hair, helping the darkness obscure her features, even though she was moving closer, kneeling beside him.

Was it that insane Mrs. Sterling?

"Everyone thinks you're a heel, Jerry," she whispered so sweetly. "A heel . . . for a heel. . . ."

And she raised the hand that held the answer to the question of why she'd been wearing only a single spiked heel. She raised that shoe like a weapon, and his eyes were wide, providing the perfect target, as that heel came slamming down into, and bursting, his right eyeball like a plump ripe grape, entering his brain, putting an end to his scheduling problems.

When the blond woman swung the spiked heel into Karmen's other eye, it was purely gratuitous, unless one were to grant the killer a sense of symmetry.

Before she left, the blond woman wiped the shoe clean on Karmen's blue-brick-patterned sports shirt, and used his body as leverage to slip the shoe on her foot. Then her high heels clicked into the darkness, and she was several minutes gone before Chris Kline, eyes on the ratings memo in his hand, entered Studio B, saying, "Here's your memo—"

But the *o* in *memo* escalated into "Oh shit," as Chris almost stumbled into the corpse, which stared at the ceiling with gouged-out bloody sockets. (Film buff that he was, Chris would later compare the body's sightless eyes to those of the farmer in *The Birds*, a reference that was lost upon Detective Hasty of the Naperville police.)

Tossing the memo, Chris ran from the studio (a fellow film buff might liken him to Stepin Fetchit, albeit a white yuppie version), screaming for help, and just plain screaming, while the piece of paper drifted like a lazy snowflake onto the late Jerry Karmen, who of course could not read the memo's bold heading: "MURDER" SHOWS BOOST RATINGS!

Chapter Nineteen

After dark, in a battered baby-blue house trailer in a trailer park across from a gravel pit on the southern edge of Ferndale, Jolene Jones—in a tight black top, black patent leather hot pants, dark nylons, and her high-heel boots—sat like an Indian on her bed.

Her valentine-shaped behind dimpling the zebra-striped bedspread, the dark-haired woman was surrounded by the images of her clown collection (figurines and dolls on knickknack shelves, a sad-eyed smiling clown painting above the bed, two sadder-eyed smiling clown pillows at her back), alternately sipping beer and taking drags from a cigarette.

On the boom box on her nightstand, a CD by a group that she followed on the local line-dancing club circuit—Patty Russo and the Country Ramblers—was playing; the song discussed the unfairness of life ("If life was fair, I'd have wheels on my car, instead of the ones underneath my house"), but to Jolene, life was suddenly starting to get its ass in gear.

She had freshened up after getting back from Naperville, feeling surprisingly awake, almost exhilarated from the exciting day. And on the three-hour ride home, she had mulled over her situation, relishing the knowledge that she had a way of getting even with that Sterling bitch while at the same time lining her own pockets.

She had dolled herself up—her sensual mouth was thick with red lipstick, her rather thin black hair piled up in pin curls for hiding under an as-yet-to-be-selected wig—for an evening at the Golden Spike; but on impulse, eager to put her profitable plan in motion, she reached for the phone book, found the number she was looking for, and punched it in.

Drawing deeply on her cigarette, she reached for the boom box dial and turned it down ("If life was fair, I'd have it all by now"), the sound of the first ring in her ear. She placed the cigarette in a Lady Luck Casino ashtray, reached for the bottle of Blue Cat beer, which she gulped a swallow from hurriedly as she heard someone answer.

A woman.

"Conway residence." A rich contralto.

"Paul Conway please."

". . . . Is he expecting your call?"

"No," Jolene said, and she was endeavoring to sound as much like a professional woman as she could, which was a stretch for someone whose highest-paying, most responsible job to date was as a clerk at a dry cleaners. "But his editor, Will Pittman, suggested I call?"

". . . . He's downstairs in his office. I'll transfer your call. Will you hold?"

"Sure I'll hold." Jolene swayed to the Ramblers, plucking the cigarette from the tray, drawing on it deeply, allowing the smoke to stream from her nostrils, dragon-like.

"Yes?" a man's voice said, finally. A pleasant, rich voice, not unlike the woman's.

"Mr. Conway?"

"This is Paul Conway."

"This is Jolene Jones."

". . . . From the TV show? Leann Jones's sister?"

"That would be me," she said with a self-satisfied smile that was only slightly less red and thick than that of the clown in the painting framed over the bed. "Mr. Conway, I'm sorry to bother you at home in the evening. But it's vital that I see you."

"Why?"

"I don't think we should discuss it over the phone," she said. Then, choosing her words carefully, overenunciating, she said, "Trust me—this is a potentially lucrative venture."

"Really."

"Really."

There was a sound that might have been Conway sighing.

Then she asked, "Could we meet tonight?"

"Well . . . I'm working against a deadline . . . if we could make it short, maybe. How about in half an hour?"

"Nine o'clock? That would be fine."

"Know where I live, Ms. Jones? How to get here?"

"I'll find it. See you then!"

She blurted a quick good-bye before he could change his mind, and hung up gleefully, unaware of course that in a better part of town, in a house that cost more than any twenty trailers in this park put together, Paul Conway was staring in amazement at the phone receiver in his hand, as if it were some foreign object.

In fact, at the very same time that Paul Conway, in his office at home, was muttering, "What's *that* about?", smirking to himself, shaking his head and returning to his computer keyboard and monitor, Jolene in her clown-appointed bedroom, in her trailer, was bounding off the bed gleefully, turning up the CD full volume. She chugged her beer, sang along, "If life was fair, life was fair," then finding the bottle empty, she dropped her mostly spent cigarette in it for a soggy, sizzling death, and ambled sexily to the dresser, watching her own curvaceous image approach.

She was proud of her body, though she had

done nothing to achieve it, no watching her diet, no working out; she was blessed with the ability to abuse herself and, as yet at least, show little or no wear or tear for the trouble. She had no sense that, unless she changed half a dozen lifestyle patterns, she faced an inevitable ten years of hardening facial features, sagging breasts, thickening thighs, and widening hips.

At twenty-seven years of age, however, Jolene Jones could still qualify for a men's magazine centerfold, unless the clown-head tattoo on her left buttock were deemed unseemly.

On the dresser was lined her wig collection, half a dozen little styrofoam blank-faced heads bearing wigs, chiefly of the big-hair country-western variety, like the red curly number she'd worn today on *The Jenny Rivers Show*. She moved along them, touching each head briefly, like a queen regarding her court.

She paused at a golden blond wig with platinum highlights, twin arcs of shimmering hair; she contemplated this, lips pursed in a smile that was almost a kiss, then said, "Not tonight."

Finally she selected a black pageboy with a sheen like new paint, and—as drooping stuffed clowns sitting along the top of the dresser mirror seemed to watch—she tugged it on and regarded her vaguely China doll–ish visage in the mirror, her painted face hovering above the anonymous nonfaces of the Styrofoam wig holders.

She blew herself a sexy kiss, and said, "Honey-bun—you just hit the lotto."

And swaying her hips sexily to no one's delight but her own, she grabbed her car keys and purse and left for her appointment.

Chapter Twenty

While Jolene Jones drove across Ferndale to the Conway home, Mrs. Sterling entertained a guest in her cozy room at Wesley House.

Sitting at the round oak table near the kitchenette, under the petals of the daisy lamp and in its soft yellow glow, Sergeant Max Anderson slouched, his white shirt cut by dark suspenders, his tie loose; he had the weary, wasted look of a man who'd worked a long hard day, which was in fact the case. Hovering over him, Mrs. Sterling poured him a cup of coffee, her blond hair pulled back in an uncharacteristic ponytail; she looked primly proper in a pale pink sweater and a pink and gray floral skirt, and as self-composed as the detective seemed frazzled.

As usual, Anderson's questioning of the

woman had not been going well; suffering from a four-alarm headache, he was about to begin his third go-round.

"You understand that Detective Hasty from Naperville will be coming around, probably tomorrow," he said.

She poured herself a cup of coffee, too, and was returning the pot to the Mr. Coffee when she said, "I was somewhere on Interstate 80, coming home, when that rude young man was killed."

"But no one saw you? You didn't stop anywhere—for gas, or food, or coffee?"

She sat, shook her head no. "Came straight home."

"No one here at Wesley House seems to have seen you, either."

"I came right to my room."

"You didn't sign in at the desk."

"I forgot to. I'm an adult, Sergeant, and rather used to coming and going as I please."

"You're required to sign in and out, aren't you?"

"Yes, but it's a rule, not a law. They're rather loose about it here. This is not a prison, Sergeant."

He shook his head, laughed once, hollowly. "You don't understand how much trouble you're in, do you?"

She cocked her head, lifted her eyebrows in the manner of a country club matron considering the latest not terribly interesting bit of gossip. "Am I, Sergeant?"

"Aw look," he said, rubbing his hand through his thick, unruly brown hair, giving his scalp a two-second massage. "Let's cut out the chitchat, lady. Witnesses saw you lose your temper with Karmen. . . ."

As if responding to a confused child, she was shaking her head no.

He karate-chopped the air, emphasizing each word: "They saw you *physically assault* the murder victim. . . ."

"I didn't assault him," she explained patiently, "I just . . . warned him."

"You choked him!"

She shrugged. "I got his attention. . . ." She smiled sweetly at the detective and sipped her coffee, then added, "Anyway, he won't be bringing charges *now*, will he?"

A short, humorless laugh huffed from the detective's chest. "You got kind of a short fuse, don't you?"

"Do I?"

"For somebody who's supposedly getting the violence medicated out of her," he said, and reached out swiftly, savagely, grabbing Mrs. Sterling by the left wrist, turning her arm palm up, and with his other hand yanking back the sleeve of her sweater.

The bump was about the size of a .45 round, a bulge in the flesh that indicated the antipsychotic implant was securely within—untampered with—and the area healed over, no redness, no inflammation, just a few flecks of dead skin to indicate that this was an invasion of her flesh, not some benign tumor or fatty deposit.

Offended but dignified, Mrs. Sterling snugged the sleeve back over the implant bump, saying, "A sudden impulse can get the best of any of us, Sergeant."

Humiliated, Anderson bent over the table with his hands covering his face, then his fingers traveled to his scalp, scratching, massaging; the headache was killing him.

"I'm sorry," he said, hoping she wouldn't report his action.

She let him twist in the silence for a while, and when she next spoke, her words were heavy with hurt and restrained anger: "Do you know what they did to me on that television program?"

"Yeah," Anderson admitted, and he was not unsympathetic. Mrs. Sterling may have been a murderer, but she was still better than the goddamn media. "Yeah, I do."

She seemed suddenly, strangely vulnerable as she asked, "Are you going to arrest me?"

"No. I don't have enough on you." He shook his head, his mouth tightening. "And anyway . . ."

Regarding him curiously, Mrs. Sterling spoke without irony. "Some of the bite seems to have gone out of your bark, Sergeant."

He leaned back, regarding her with similar curiosity. "Your shrink says these murders aren't your style."

"What do *you* think?"

He stood, sighed, and, thumbs in his belt loops, he hovered over her as he said carefully, "I think if you decided to kill that sleazeball, you wouldn't tip your hand in front of a studio audience. . . ."

She smiled up at him, nodding just a little.

"And," he continued, looking down at her but not talking down to her, "you wouldn't have gouged his eyes out with your spiked heel, either—too messy."

She smiled some more, agreeing by shaking her head, no.

Then she spoke in a clear, cool voice, looking up at him with clear, cool eyes. "If I were the person you think I am . . . and I'm not, I'm completely innocent, never have and never would intentionally kill anyone . . ."

"Never," Anderson smiled.

She shrugged. "I'd have made it look like an accident. I'd have made sure that falling light put *his* lights out . . . *if* I were the person you think I am."

Anderson, smiling, nodding, ambled toward the nubby brown sofa, where he plucked from the end table a framed photo of Mrs. Sterling and Jessica Ann in happier days.

"Well," he said, regarding the photo, "you and me and your head doctor know this MO is all wrong for you. . . ." Then he smiled cutely over at her. "But that doesn't mean you won't wind up taking the fall."

Alarmed, Mrs. Sterling said, "But I didn't do these murders."

"Oh, but you never did *any* murders, remember?" His headache was suddenly gone. "You're just a poor, innocent mom . . ."

And he held up the gilt-framed photo of mother and daughter for her perusal, adding, ". . . who somebody's putting in a very fancy frame."

Anderson put the picture back as Mrs. Sterling, frowning in thought, finally appeared to know just how much trouble she was in.

Chapter Twenty-one

In his large office in the finished basement of the white split-level house he shared with his wife and niece, Paul Conway sat at his mahogany desk in the green glow of his computer screen, fingers flying at the keyboard as he worked against deadline for a piece he was writing for *Playboy*.

It was a reconsideration of Truman Capote's classic *In Cold Blood*, a book Conway dearly loved (a dog-eared copy was near his notes, on the desk); Capote had virtually invented the non-fiction novel style from which the entire "true crime" genre had emerged. And the effete, fearless Capote had also been so bold as to insert himself into the story, getting to know the convicted murderers and, with his presence in the narrative, providing his book with a powerful third act.

Conway had a real sense of history where his field was concerned; around him on his cream-colored office walls hung framed original cover paintings of 1950s vintage crime books and "true detective" magazines, purchased from auction at Christie's—pulpy, campily garish images of gangsters and gun molls, of tough men and loose women. On the sparse wall space that his desk faced (a partial wall, bisected into a triangle to make way for the open stairway) were hung various framed awards and mementos—framed certificates for Edgar and Shamus award nominations, original pasteups of the covers of his books, *The Mommy Murders* and *Conversations with Killers*, and his own smiling face on the cover of *Mystery Scene* magazine.

For a writer, his work area was well organized and tidy, his desk distinguished by a Sherlock Holmes mug and a gold, dagger-style letter opener presented to him by the International Crime Writers League. On the mahogany two-drawer file that matched the desk resided the ugly little porcelain bust of Edgar Allan Poe that represented his award from the Mystery Writers of America for *The Mommy Murders* ("Best True Crime Book"). Also atop the file was a plaster statue of a black bird, a replica of the Maltese Falcon from that famous film; and a smiling framed black-and-white portrait of his wife, Beth.

Movement on the stairway caught his attention and he leaned back and watched two pairs of attractive female legs coming down—the first pair belonged, no doubt, to the guest he was expecting, Jolene Jones, and they were well shaped and well displayed beneath black patent leather hot pants, and encased in dark but sheer nylons; the second pair of gams, equally fetching, bare under denim shorts, belonged to his wife.

Soon they were at the bottom of the stairs, Jolene Jones looking like a cocktail waitress in her tight black short-sleeve sweater designed to show off an impressive swell of bosom, with a faintly smirking Beth just behind her, girlish in a floral vest and T-shirt.

"You have such a lovely home, Mrs. Conway," Jolene was saying with syrupy Eddie Haskel–style sincerity. "You must be very proud."

"Thank you," Beth said. Then, with their voluptuous guest's back to her, his wife arched her eyebrows and to Conway added, "Let me know if you need anything."

Beth headed up the stairs, twitching her trim behind as she went as if to remind Conway of what he already had at home. Then the writer smiled politely at his guest, not getting up, swiveling to gesture to a waiting chair by his file cabinet, saying, "Sit down, Ms. Jones."

But she already had.

"Call me Jolene, would you? I don't stand on formalities." She was digging in her black patent leather purse. "You mind if I smoke?"

"Actually, yes," Conway said, leaning back in his chair, keeping his distance from his attractive, if slutty looking caller. "My wife doesn't allow smoking in the house."

She snapped her purse shut, glancing up with amusement. "I would have guessed *you* were in charge around here. . . . It was your 'Mommy' book that paid for all this, wasn't it?"

He sighed. Forced a smile. "Ms. Jones . . . Jolene . . . I'm on a deadline. Out of courtesy to you, and your late sister's memory, I—"

"My 'late sister' was trash," she smirked. With those full, overly lipsticked lips, there was something obscene about it. "I think she was a dyke or somethin'. . . . Now, me, myself . . ." And she damn near leered at him, eyes moving up and down him as if he were a new tacky outfit she were considering trying on. ". . . I got more . . . conventional tastes."

He crossed his legs, already bored with her. "Please get to the point, Jolene."

She leaned closer, confiding in him. "Point is, reality don't count for nothin'—appearance is all."

"You don't say."

"That's exactly what I say." She shrugged. "Look at all these TV shows I been doin'. It don't matter if my sister and me ain't spoke since high school. . . ."

"Then why don't you tell me what does matter?"

Jolene didn't reply. Instead, she glanced past

him at his framed book covers on his wall; not the vintage stuff, but his own work, *The Mommy Murders, Conversations with Killers.* Almost to herself, she said, "I'm an author, too, you know."

"Really?"

Now she gazed at him, her eyes hooded. "I wasn't lyin' about your editor when I called—him and five others . . . they *all* want me."

Now he leered at her. "For what?"

She scooted her chair closer, chummy, conspiratorial. "Soon as the cops nail your looney sister-in-law for these new murders, there's gonna be room for *another* Mommy book on the best-seller list."

Conway couldn't suppress his smile. "And *you're* going to write it?"

She put a black-nailed hand on his leg. "Why don't *we* write it . . . together?"

Now he edged toward her, so close he could have kissed that lush red mouth.

"I get it," he said. "With your charisma—on the talk show circuit—and my name next to yours on the cover . . ."

"Sequel to a best-seller," she whispered dreamily.

Her lips were very near his.

"I bet we'd work really well together," she said.

"You know, I just thought of something," he said intimately.

"Yeah?" she asked suggestively, as if expecting a page out of the Kama Sutra. "What?"

"My wife doesn't allow animals in the house

either. . . ." Still close enough to kiss her, he gazed right into her eyes and smiled as he said, "Take a fuckin' hike."

She scooted back, shot to her feet, and her shapely form was blurring by him as she huffed, "I don't need you to do this. This was just . . . professional courtesy."

What, he thought, *one whore to another?*

But he said nothing. He just watched her stride up the stairs, and couldn't help but admire that nice body on that rotten woman.

Neither of them had been aware that Jessica Ann, already dressed for bed in her hot pink pajamas, having seen Jolene arrive, had heard much of this conversation. She had knelt at the landing and peeked around the corner and, above them, watched Jolene, heard Jolene, saw Jolene touch Paul's leg and almost kiss him, almost laughing out loud when Paul rebuffed her.

And when Jolene had risen so quickly, heading for the stairs, Jessica Ann had scurried away, up the short flight of stairs and through the house and into her bedroom, where she knelt by her bed, hurriedly punching in a number on the nightstand phone, a number she had never called before, although she had it memorized.

"Hello?" her mother's voice said.

"Mommy!"

In her room at Wesley House, wearing the green robe she had shot Mark Jeffries in two years before, Mrs. Sterling held the phone in one hand and a cigarette in the other; her eyes were alive with surprise and joy. "Jessica Ann?"

"Mommy," her daughter's whispered voice was saying, "I just saw that terrible woman . . . I heard her say a lot of awful things."

And, crouched beside her bed like a bandit, the girl reported the conversation, as best she could remember, to her mother.

"You know what I think?" the girl asked.

"What, dear?"

"I think she could be the one doing this. The one making it look like you're killing people . . ." Jessica Ann almost said "again," but caught herself.

"Yes," her mother's voice was saying thoughtfully, "she *could* be the one doing this to Mommy. . . . Dear?"

"Yes, Mommy?"

"It means so much to me, you calling me like this."

"I know. . . . I have to go. Aunt Beth will kill me if she catches me talking to you."

And the child hung up.

At Wesley House, the woman in the green robe hung up and for a moment just sat there quietly, a tiny smile tickling her lips, as she basked in the afterglow of her daughter's words.

Then the words themselves began to sink in, to really take root, and Mrs. Sterling frowned, knowing there was something she must do.

Tonight.

205

Chapter Twenty-two

Jolene Jones, novice author that she was, did not realize how presumptuous it was for her to call her editor, Will Pittman, at home, at night. Nor did she factor in the difference in time zones, nor was she aware just how rare it was for a New York editor to give out his or her home number to an author. When they had negotiated the book contract in a hotel in Chicago last month, however, certain concessions had been made.

Wearing nothing but a thin cotton floral-print robe and big brown furry moose slippers with moving eyes and floppy ears, Jolene—her long, rather thin dark hair bouncing on her shoulders, and prettier than any wig she owned (though she did not realize that)—sat on her bed in her trailer, surrounded by clown images, smoking as she talked on the phone.

She had already told the editor the good news about the TV producer's murder—another killing to stir the public's interest, and beef up the plot (and violence quotient) of their book.

"Listen, do we really need that Conway?" she was asking.

"Not really," Pittman said patiently. His young-sounding second tenor–ish voice brought his pleasant good looks to her mind as they spoke. He was the youngest senior editor at the prestigious publishing house.

"I didn't think so," Jolene said cockily, blowing out smoke.

"But of course, with Conway out, we'll need to consider bringing in a ghostwriter."

"You mean like Stephen King?"

There was a pause, filled by a sound that might have been suppressed laughter, which puzzled Jolene. Had she said something funny?

"No, uh, it's a professional writer who can help you get your thoughts organized."

"Oh. How does that work?"

"Sort of like an interview. The 'ghost' will record your thoughts, and sort of rearrange and spruce up the material, so it reads like a book."

"Oh! Then I just talk into a tape?"

"That's right. I mean, Jolene, you don't have any writing experience. We have to pay a professional to—"

"How *much* do we have to pay?" she frowned.

"It won't be exorbitant. Ten thousand dollars, maybe, and a small royalty."

"Does that come out of my end?"

"Yes, but it won't cost near as much as having Conway aboard, doing the actual writing. He's a name author; he would have wanted at least fifty percent of the action, maybe more."

"Yeah," Jolene said, nodding thoughtfully, "I guess he woulda took a big bite, what with that best-seller and all."

"Precisely."

"Then maybe we're better off?"

"Maybe we're better off."

"Yeah!" She bounced on the bed like a kid. "So, when do we start?"

"Well, I don't see any reason to wait for Mrs. Sterling's arrest and trial."

Jolene leaned back against her colorful clown pillows, making her face one of three red-mouthed faces all lined up together. "They'll close in on her soon enough," she told the editor, "don't worry about that."

"Well, my thinking is, get started on the book so that the hardcover can be in the stores when the trial's under way, and then we can do a new, 'bonus update' chapter on the trial's outcome for the paperback. So then, I'd say whenever you're ready."

Jolene had just blown a smoke ring and was grinning as she watched it drift and dissolve. "Baby, I was born ready."

"Then I'll line up your ghostwriter and get you two together with a tape recorder."

"Okay!"

"Okay, Jolene. Good talking to you."

"Okay," she said, exhilarated by this wonderful business conference, "bye-bye."

The Ringling Brothers–like clown image on the pillow next to her had a hand poised in a white-gloved wave. The artist had probably intended a wave of hello, but the sad-eyed clown seemed to be waving good-bye as Jolene sat up, drawing deeply on the smoke, filling her lungs. She held the smoke there, then exhaled as she hugged her legs, and seemed to be speaking to the moose slippers as she looked down, saying, "Who needs ya, ya stuck-up jerk," meaning Conway, who she then mocked with, " 'My wife don't allow smokin' in the house' . . . and I bet that ain't the only thing."

Smirking, she took one last draw and leaned over toward the nightstand to drop the cigarette sizzlingly into her latest mostly drained bottle of Blue Cat beer, and slid off the bed, padding in her moose slippers toward the bathroom.

"Money money money money money money," she sang tunelessly to herself.

The bathroom, all white and yellow, was small, though large for a trailer, with a shower-curtained tub; she'd cleaned the bathroom yesterday, and the yellow rubber gloves and can of Comet cleanser were still by the sink, her boom box sitting atop the toilet tank, its silver speakers like two big eyes that made a face out of the toilet. She'd been listening to music—another local band, T-Bone Thomas and his Rockabilly Band, a tape not a CD—while she cleaned the bathroom, but didn't bother plugging it in and turning it on now—she'd never hear it over the sound of her shower.

She slipped out of her robe and it puddled at her feet, near a clown-head rug; she glanced at herself in the mirror, admiring the tilt of her breasts—C-cup but no droop at all, not bad!—and then looked back over her shoulder at herself in the glass, admiring her pretty back tapering to the narrow waist and cute little dimples over the upside-down valentine behind. She blew herself a kiss, saying, "You heartbreaker you," stepped out of her moose slippers and into the tub.

She turned the shower knob, adjusted the spray for the lukewarm temperature she liked—she was not one for a hot, steamy shower—and stood beneath the needles of water, soaping herself. Within the stall of the tub-shower combo, the water spray was loud, echoey, and she did not hear the blond woman come in, despite the click of the spiked heels.

Nor did Jolene, her back to the translucent shower curtain, see the blond woman—country club stylish in a severe lavender pantsuit—move to the sink, where she discovered the yellow rubber gloves. The sink and toilet were to one side of the tub, so when Jolene did turn, she saw nothing, heard nothing, then as Jolene stuck her head under the nozzle, applying shampoo, scrubbing her hair, she removed herself further from any possibility of noticing the intruder.

Who was kneeling now, below the sink, looking for the makings of an improvised course of action. Nothing useful under there. But in one of the drawers, the blond woman found a wrapped, brown extension cord.

And as Jolene rinsed her hair, the blond woman tugged on the rubber gloves, unwrapped the extension cord, and plugged it into a wall socket, next to the mirror, near the toilet.

The first indication Jolene had that she had company was when the shower curtain was yanked rudely back. The wet, naked woman turned toward the sound, startled, her mouth dropping like a trapdoor, and she saw the vague shape of the blond woman, but before her wet eyes could focus, Jolene realized the woman was flinging something toward her.

Reflexively, Jolene caught the boom box, clutched it, and in so doing, her fingers inadvertently punched PLAY, the tape starting up, accompanied by the *zzzzzzzzzzsst* of electricity, her wide, paralyzed eyes not seeing the blond woman holding the plug into the wall as Jolene's body seemed to dance to the music. . . .

First ya start to tingle, then you start to shake . . . as the naked woman convulsed, *zzzzzzzzzzsst*, the electrical shock making her shimmy . . .

Lightnin' bolt strike ya, inhibitions start to break . . . and the high voltage ruptured the electrical circuit in her heart, its beat stopping, *zzzzzzzzzzsst*, though her feet seemed to keep the beat of the music . . .

Your blood starts to boil, and your knees begin to quiver . . . and with her mouth open in its silent scream, Jolene seemed to be singing along, *zzzzzzzzzzsst*, as the blond woman's rubber-gloved hand held that plug in the outlet, *zzzzzzzzzzsst*, keeping the extension cord pulled taut . . .

Your mind shorts in and out and your body starts to shiver . . . as smoke and sparks mingled with the shower water drumming down, *zzzzzzzzzzsst*, Jolene clutching that boom box to her bosom as if covering herself modestly . . .

You got that all-over tingle and you're actin' kind of silly . . . and as her feet finally stopped dancing, *zzzzzzzzzzsst*, Jolene—shivering, as if having taken a chill—began to slide down the stall, *zzzzzzzzzzsst*, her thin wet hair trailing behind her like seaweed . . .

You got the high-voltage blues, and you dance the shockabilly, dance the—

But the music was over, the plug yanked out of its socket, T-Bone Thomas and his Rockabilly Band ejecting in a spiral of half-eaten tape, as Jolene, a lump of steaming meat in the corner of the tub, her breasts still covered modestly by the boom box in hands that had finally gone limp, sat staring with bulging eyes that had nearly burst from the thousands of volts that had passed through her pale wet body.

The blond woman tossed the gloves and extension cord on the clown rug, the eyes of the moose slippers the only witnesses as she stalked out, while down the drain of the tub curled strands of Jolene's dark, thinning hair.

Chapter Twenty-three

Jessica Ann was dreaming. She had told no one, not even Uncle Paul, of the recurring dream, which she was in the midst of right now.

She was back in the junkyard, on that terrible night, under the charcoal-streaked moon; but she wasn't fearfully fleeing her mother. In fact, her mother was at her side and they were walking hand in hand, moving up and down the street-like paths of the junkyard, looking at the crushed cars and dead refrigerators and rusty steel drums, oohing and aahing, as if they were in a particularly fascinating museum.

Usually that was the whole dream, a meandering stroll through the junkyard that sometimes evolved into a wholly other dream, as dreams are wont to do; but tonight was different. Tonight the dream continued as Mommy and Jessica Ann heard something, someone behind them, and a dark figure, just a shape, was moving after them, stalking them, and now Mommy and Jessica Ann ran, hand in hand, both screaming like scared children, as the mummy-like monster pursued them.

And when they were finally cornered against the Stonehenge-like pile of dead cars, helpless victims hugging each other and waiting for a dire fate, right before the monster could step into the moonlight and reveal its identity, Jessica Ann drifted into a half-waking state, with a vague awareness that she was safe in her bed in the Conway home.

Only a figure in the darkness was moving in over her, and it was no dream, not the pair of outstretched hands emerging into the moonlight filtering through a high bedroom window, hands with graceful, tapering fingers with lovely red nails.

The girl came fully awake with a start, as the pale cameo of her mother's face, framed by golden arcs of hair, moved into the moonlight and one hand moved past the girl's throat to stroke her face gently, as Mommy said, "Jessica Ann . . . dear . . . wake up."

But she was already wide awake, and stunned by her mother's presence. "Mommy . . . ?"

Mommy was sitting on the bed, leaning over her daughter in the near darkness, whispering, "I'm leaving, dear."

Alarmed by this news, Jessica Ann half sat up, leaning on an elbow, trying to comprehend. "Leaving?"

Mommy nodded. "We both know I didn't do those things. I know you believe me . . . and that means so much to me."

"I know, Mommy."

"You know, too, that someone's making it look like Mommy," she said, shaking her head woefully. Mommy was good at martyrdom; maybe all mothers were. "And there's nothing I can do. . . ."

"Can't Mr. Ekhardt help you?"

"Not this time, not this time. Now, I have some money hidden, under a new name, and . . . I'm going to leave the country."

Jessica Ann felt overwhelmed by all this news; she shook her head, as if to clear it, saying, "Will I ever see you . . . ?"

That response seemed to surprise Mommy. "You don't understand . . . I want you to come with me."

The enormity of that suggestion staggered the child. Head reeling, she whispered, "Oh, Mommy . . ."

Mommy took one of Jessica Ann's hands in hers like a suitor proposing marriage and said, "We can start over. Clean. Fresh. A second chance . . ."

This was the mother she had always longed for: as loving as she was beautiful, a mother with a face filled with nothing but love for Jessica Ann.

Flooded with joy, the child whispered, "Oh, Mommy . . ."

Taking this as a yes, Mommy smiled the dazzling smile. "Can you quietly get a few of your things together? We can slip out through the downstairs—"

And a click that sounded like the cocking of a big gun was actually the light switch, and the room filled with harsh illumination, mother and daughter caught in the glare, conspirators nabbed by a coldly furious Aunt Beth, her pretty face contorted by a sneer.

"I want you out of here," Aunt Beth told Mommy, glaring daggers at her. "Now."

Jessica Ann had clutched her mommy, was hugging her.

Near tears, Mommy said, "Please, Beth . . . she's my baby. . . ."

Bitterness edged Aunt Beth's words. "You want me to call the police?"

But coming up behind her was Uncle Paul, looking concerned; he slipped an arm around his wife's shoulder, and looked beyond her to the mother and daughter huddling pitifully on the bed.

"I don't think you'd better call anybody right now," Uncle Paul advised Aunt Beth. He curled a finger at Mommy and Jessica Ann, gestured with a jerk of his head. "Ladies—we'd better talk."

Aunt Beth didn't argue, allowed her husband to walk away from the girl's bedroom, as Jessica

Ann in her hot pink pajamas helped her mother off the bed. Beth looked like a pouting kid in her cutoff jeans and T-shirt and little floral vest; Mommy was wearing a black sweater with a few colorful dancing tulips on it and a full, flowing black skirt with *lots* of colorful dancing tulips on it. Mommy and Jessica Ann held hands as they followed Paul and Beth to the living room.

Soon the three females were on the uncomfortable green Queen Anne couch, Mommy in the middle, Jessica Ann at left, grasping her mother's hand, Beth sitting as far away from her sister as possible, while Uncle Paul pulled a chair from somewhere and sat backwards on it.

He patted the air with a cautionary palm. "Now, I want everyone to stay nice and calm. . . . We're all friends here . . . we're all family. . . ."

Aunt Beth frowned. "What's happened now?"

He sighed. "Well, what with everything that's been going on, I've been monitoring the police-band radio in my office . . ."

"What did you hear?" Beth demanded.

Jessica Ann, worried, squeezed her mother's hand supportively. Mommy seemed almost woozy, as if her medication was too strong.

"Jolene Jones has been murdered," Uncle Paul said.

And Jessica Ann, the old fear, the old guilt surging through her, withdrew her hand from her mother's, as if that hand had suddenly gone hot as a kitchen burner on high.

Scooting away from her mother, shaking her

head, Jessica Ann said apologetically, "It's my fault . . . I shouldn't have called you. . . . I'm so sorry, I'm so sorry. . . ."

Mommy leaned toward the girl, the lovely face twisted with anguish. "No, baby, I didn't do it. . . ." Taking the girl's face in both hands, she turned her daughter gently toward her; Jessica Ann's eyes were wild. "Please, please, dear. . . . You have to believe me. . . ."

Uncle Paul spoke directly to Mommy. "There's a warrant out for your arrest."

Mommy turned toward Uncle Paul as Aunt Beth demanded, "What *happened*?"

Uncle Paul swallowed and, almost reluctantly, very quietly, said, "She was electrocuted."

And as both Jessica Ann and Beth pulled even further away from her on the couch, gazing at her with hard-eyed suspicion, Mommy shook her head, no, no, no.

"Someone entered her trailer," he said. "Some kind of radio or something, plugged into the wall, was thrown into her shower."

"It wasn't me," Mommy said, gesturing to herself with both hands, pitifully pleading her case, turning from her sister then to her daughter, hoping to find a sympathetic court in one of them. "I swear it wasn't me. I haven't been murdering these people. . . . I'm *innocent*!"

Then she began to cry, muttering, "You've got to believe me. . . ."

Jessica Ann didn't know what to do; she wanted to comfort her mother, but how could she believe her after everything that had happened? Aunt Beth seemed to be wavering, too; but she kept her distance.

Mommy was alone.

Uncle Paul said, "I think you should call your attorney." He had a portable phone and was holding it out to her in a sort of peace offering. "You remember his home number?"

Mommy nodded, dabbing her eyes with her handkerchief, pulling herself together, taking the phone. She drew several deep breaths, searched her mind for the number, and punched it in.

It rang five times and then the familiar, husky voice, answered, "This is Neal Ekhardt . . ."

"Neal," she began. She was toying nervously with the gold cross at her throat.

But it was his answering machine. "I'm out of town. I will be checking my messages."

Mommy looked up from the receiver, panicky. "It's his machine!" She looked from Paul to Beth. "Should I leave a message? Can I . . . can I have him call me here?"

Aunt Beth was thinking that over; she looked to her husband, who nodded his consent. Then Beth turned to her sister and quietly said, "Yes."

Relieved, Mommy said into the phone, "Neal— this is . . . you know who this is. It's urgent we talk. I'm at my sister's."

Disconnecting, she handed the phone back to Paul, thanking him, then turned to Beth and thanked her as well.

Mommy looked at Aunt Beth beseechingly.

"Could I . . . use the spare bedroom?"

Aunt Beth looked at Uncle Paul, who again nodded his approval, and then something amazing happened. Aunt Beth smiled at Mommy. Not a big smile, but a real smile, and Beth said, "Yes . . . yes, stay with us. We'll get this sorted out."

Then Mommy broke into tears and Aunt Beth was crying too, although more quietly, as the two sisters embraced, Beth patting Mommy on the back, there there, there there.

Suddenly this nightmare had a happy ending; Jessica Ann felt a surge of warmth as renewed faith flowed through her—*Mommy* didn't do these murders—and she looked at Uncle Paul, who had kept his promise and brought them all back together, and he smiled, just a little, and gave her the thumbs-up.

Jessica Ann, joining the embrace, turning it into a three-way hug, returned the thumbs-up even as the tears streamed down her apple cheeks.

Chapter Twenty-four

The morning—early enough for a papergirl to glide by, flinging a Des Moines *Register* at the porch of the Conway home—was idyllic: birds chirping a chipper symphony, an easy spring breeze fluttering the well-tended shrubbery that hugged the white split-level, the rays of the sun as golden as butter dripping down breakfast pancakes.

Within her curtained bedroom, however, Jessica Ann did not stir; on the nightstand, the clock read 6:29. In cool darkness, the girl was sleeping deeply, and working the sounds of the morning birds into her dream, which was of a sunny day very much like this one. She was on a family picnic with her mother and father, although sometimes Daddy was Mark Jeffries and other times he was Uncle Paul, but mostly he was Daddy. Aunt Beth was not in the dream.

Jessica Ann was not aware of the figure creeping into her bedroom, nor did she even open her eyes when the blond woman leaned in with the chloroform-soaked cloth. Only when the cloth had been fitted over her mouth, and the girl involuntarily sucked in the strong, medicinal fumes, did her eyes pop open wide, though in the darkness all she could make out were the swinging scythe blades of golden hair.

Her struggle was only momentary, before the girl dropped into a dreamless darkness.

Elsewhere in the house, Beth Conway slept, and for the first time in the days since her sister's release, she had not slept fitfully. She, too, had tranquil dreams, and her sister was in them, a smiling, playful sister that only existed in Beth's dreams, and lately, not even there.

But last night's tearful reunion had triggered within the woman dormant feelings, the old longings for a normal, loving family life that included a sister whose behavior was as lovely as her dazzling smile. Since childhood, that fantasy sister had been a regular player in the repertory company of Beth's dream playhouse, and in this dream they were back in high school, and Beth was going to the homecoming dance in a new dress loaned to her by her loving sister. (This was a revision of reality, as what her sister had really done was thoughtlessly wear Beth's new dress to school on the day of the homecoming dance.)

The sound of a car door shutting and then that car pulling away stirred Beth, and she sat up, glancing at the nightstand clock—7:05—and at her husband, slumbering peacefully next to her. Other neighborhood sounds—including a lawn mower from somewhere down the street—announced the new day was seriously under way; but the sleeping Paul was oblivious. He could sleep through a train wreck, Beth thought wryly as she stepped out of bed, pulling her nightshirt up over her slim, shapely body, the air-conditioning perking the nipples of her girlish breasts.

The slamming car door, the car pulling away, had not quite alarmed her, but the sounds had been just outside the house, and with a fugitive like her sister as a houseguest, Beth felt a sudden urge to check up on Jessica Ann and her mother. She didn't bother with underwear, stepping into her jeans, pulling the purple sweatshirt down over her head, shaking the mane of her long dark hair as she headed into the hallway.

The guest room was empty—the bed neatly made. No sign of her sister. Beth's heart began to race and her stomach churned, prevomit saliva racing into a mouth already nasty with morning aftertaste.

Maybe she got lonely in the night for Jessica Ann, Beth thought desperately, *and came in and curled up beside her. . . .*

But in the girl's bedroom, Beth found neither mother nor daughter. Leaning in, eyes wildly searching the room, Beth discovered covers thrown rudely back, and near the pillow—still cleaved with the impression of the child's sleeping head—lay a small, crumpled cloth. Beth picked it up and sniffed it, and the stench of chloroform rose like industrial smoke and brought tears to her eyes.

She ran from the room and quickly searched the house, every room, even the garage.

Her sister's red Sunbird was gone.

Though her footsteps had surely echoed through the house like an elephant stampede, she found her husband still peacefully snoozing; she shook him violently.

"What?" he asked sleepily.

"They're gone," she said.

Now he was instantly awake, face distorted with bewilderment. "Gone?"

Together they searched the house again, and outside they went to the neighbors on either side and across the way to see if anyone had seen anything. No one had.

Paul got the coffee while Beth made the phone call.

"I don't think the little girl's in any danger." Sergeant Anderson's voice, over the phone, was both strong and reassuring.

But it wasn't enough.

"How can you say that? You know what she did in the junkyard!"

"That was a long time ago," Anderson's voice returned reasonably. "We both know what's motivating her now. She wants her daughter back."

"You've got to do something!"

"We both know she loves that little girl. . . ."

"I know she tried to kill her once!" Paul had delivered a cup of coffee to her, but Beth ignored it. "Jessica Ann didn't go willingly—that cloth was soaked in chloroform! This is a kidnapping!"

"Now, please, Mrs. Conway, please—I'm going to get an APB out on both of them. . . ."

"This is exactly what she did last time! She grabbed Jessy and ran!"

"I know, I know. But it's always tricky when a parent takes a child. . . . It's technically kidnapping, but—"

"I've got a court order keeping her away!"

"Yes, and you let your sister in your home last night, didn't you? Near that child?"

"You're not blaming *me* for this?" Beth's indignation rang hollow; she was already blaming herself.

"No. But you were harboring a fugitive. . . ."

"Well, then, by all means, come over and arrest me! Don't bother looking for my sister and the little girl she chloroformed and kidnapped!"

"Please, Mrs. Conway . . . please. Settle down. I need you to do me a favor. Can you do that?"

"What favor?"

"If you'll recall, the last time your sister fled, she was planning to leave the country. So we're going to want to hit the airports, bus lines, trains . . . I need a photo of Jessica Ann. Can you get me that right away?"

"A photo. But not one of my sister?"

"No. We're covered on that score. Just the girl. Can you do that?"

"Yes, Sergeant."

"You want me to send an officer after it?"

"No, I'll be right down."

Beth hit END on the portable phone; she was sitting at the round table in the dining nook of the kitchen. Sun streamed through the nearby calico-curtained windows, turning the open-beamed, pine-paneled room golden and decorating the maple table with the patterns of the tree leaves that the sun rays had found their way between.

"He needs a photograph of Jessica Ann to distribute," Beth said numbly, but Paul—in gray T-shirt, cutoff jeans and sandals—was already plucking a beaming snapshot of the girl from its magnet on the refrigerator. He handed it to Beth.

"He has plenty of my sister already," she said wryly.

He smiled patiently. "You go. I'll hold down the fort here."

She nodded, swallowed. Rising, she leaned toward him and gave him a kiss.

"What would I do without you?" she asked.

"It's never gonna come up," he said with a little grin. "Go. I'll stick by the phone."

She went out the kitchen door that led into the garage and their waiting BMW, and her husband—coffee cup in hand—went downstairs, to his office, where he switched on his computer, to work and keep vigil.

Chapter Twenty-five

Five minutes or so after Beth Conway left for the Public Safety Building, Mrs. Sterling—returning from the supermarket with a grocery bag filled with the makings of the surprise breakfast she had planned for the family—pulled her red Sunbird into the garage, unaware that her daughter had been kidnapped, or that she was the only suspect in the crime.

She was surprised to find the BMW gone, and wondered whether it was Beth or Paul or both of them who had taken it, and where they'd gone off to; but read nothing ominous into it. The other family car, a gold and black Jeep Cherokee, was still in its stall.

She wore a white summer suit over a beige shell top that seemed at once formal and sporty;

she had selected the elegant ensemble, a past favorite of hers, from the bag she'd hastily packed at Wesley House yesterday, choosing it over her more softly feminine, floral attire of recent days, because the suit's severe yet stylish lines suddenly seemed more *her*: the strong image she wished to present for her daughter, softened by angelic white.

Shutting the car door with her hip, her arms juggling the overflowing bag, out of which peeked pancake mix, an egg carton, and a jug of orange juice, she groped in her purse for the house key. It was the same key she'd used to get in the night before, found under the backdoor welcome mat, where she knew it was her sister's habit to leave one. Soon she stood at the door from the garage to the kitchen, fumbling with the key at the lock even as the phone rang just beyond.

Neal, she thought, buoyed by the thought of having her trusted attorney's counsel.

She entered, beaming, setting the bag of groceries down on the maple table, snatching up the portable phone after the second ring, hitting the button, hearing Paul picking up simultaneously, saying, "Yes?"

He must have been in his office downstairs, working.

And, before she could speak, Mrs. Sterling heard a second voice on the phone, and it wasn't Neal Ekhardt, either; it was a woman's voice, a hard-edged voice that was not familiar to her.

230

"I've got the brat," the woman said.

Jessica Ann's mother felt as though she'd been struck a blow; she instinctively knew not to say anything. Just to listen, which she did in wide-eyed alarm.

"You know what to do," Conway's voice said.

There was a coldness in his voice that was new to Mrs. Sterling and yet somehow made perfect sense, somehow confirmed a suspicion about the man who'd profited from the Sterling family's misery, a foreboding that had lurked in the recesses of her mind, numbed by the drug coursing through her veins.

"I want more," the woman said, as cold and nasty as a spoiled child.

Mrs. Sterling, head reeling, almost fell into a chair, hand covering the mouthpiece. Listening.

"More what?" Conway asked, irritated.

"More whaddya think? *Money*, dickweed! You want this kid dead, I want a percentage!"

It was a good thing she had her palm over the mouthpiece, because at these latest unexpected words, Mrs. Sterling sucked in air in shock.

"A percentage?" Conway said, incredulity thick in his tone.

"You're gonna make a bundle off this little sequel you plotted," the woman said smugly. "*I'm* the one doin' the scut work."

Anger and fear whirled within Jessica Ann's mother. Still listening, she walked with the portable phone in hand, mouthpiece covered, to the girl's bedroom, saw the mussed sheets and blankets, sniffed the chloroformed rag, and understood.

Understood everything.

"I want it *in writing*," the woman was telling the man who'd hired her to play Mommy. "A piece of the book, the movie . . . who knows? Maybe they'll do a CD-ROM, Mommy chasin' baby around with a butcher knife . . ."

And the real Mommy sneered at this, rage boiling within her, but said nothing; just listened.

"You want me to put a murder contract in writing?" Conway asked her, obviously flabbergasted by the woman's brazen blackmail. "Are you completely out of your mind?"

Mrs. Sterling had moved back into the kitchen, and again sat at the table, her groceries nearby, as she eavesdropped on the bizarre conversation, eyes wide, pulse racing.

"I'm a consultant," the woman said haughtily. "I want it in writing, and I want it *now*."

There was a long pause, and finally Paul's voice, the familiar, reasonable voice, asked, "Where are you?"

"Where we made the first money drop," the woman said. "Remember?"

A suggestiveness in her tone made Mrs. Sterling wonder if there'd been something personal between Conway and his employee.

"All right," Conway said wearily.

"Won't take you half an hour," the woman said. "At least . . . it better not."

A click signaled the woman had hung up, and

then so did Conway and, carefully, Mrs. Sterling did too.

In his basement office, surrounded by pulp painting images of betraying women and male patsies, harlots and heels, vixens and louses, Conway sat in the green glow of his computer screen and contemplated his next move. On the desk, near his letter opener and Sherlock Holmes mug, was the note he'd scribbled to himself: *Old Mill Park*. That's where they'd met for the first money drop. She must have called him from that rest stop at the park, near where he'd parked the Jeep and sweatily sealed their bargain in the backseat.

While Conway gathered his thoughts downstairs, Mrs. Sterling was almost directly above him, pacing near the kitchen table, nervously fingering her gold necklace, rubbing the cross as if for luck, or guidance. She was almost dizzy with conflicting emotions, the bubbling rage within her unable to flush out the sense of unsureness, the anxiety that manifested itself in trembling and unfocused thought, fears for her daughter making her tearful, a desire for vengeance, an urge for immediate action, kept in abeyance by doubts and misgivings, even as some contract murderer held her beloved daughter hostage until the man who'd hired her came up with more money. . . .

This was no time for doubts, for misgivings, for wondering what was right or wrong. This was a time for Jessica Ann's mommy to listen to her natural instincts, and to do that, she needed to purge herself of that foul foreign object within her, for she too was held hostage. . . .

A savage impulse breaking through all caution, Mrs. Sterling scowled, left eye twitching, as she clutched the gold cross and yanked, snapping the chain around her neck; then with her right hand, still grasping the cross, she feverishly drew back the sleeve of the white suit jacket, baring her forearm, like a junkie about to shoot up.

But Jessica Ann's mommy wasn't injecting herself; she had to remove the restraining drugs from her system. The gold cross had a rugged surface, and its tip was somewhat pointed, even jagged, and it served as a makeshift tool as she pierced the flesh at the base of the implant bump, and a teardrop of blood wept from the cut she made, a slit in her skin little more than a quarter of an inch wide.

Downstairs, in his office, Conway had decided on a course of action. He moved to the two-drawer file, atop of which the framed photo of his wife watched mutely with a smile of seeming approval, and he knelt before the cabinet like an altar. He pulled out the bottom drawer and fished beneath some boxed manuscripts for the .38 Colt revolver.

Upstairs, Mrs. Sterling was picking at the opening in her arm as if it were a scab, her long nails seeking the tip of the projectile-like implant, trying to edge it out of its sheath of skin enough for her to get ahold of it. She panted from the effort and the pain; it was like trying to re-move a particularly disagreeable splinter. Blood trickled but did not pour, an annoyance in that it made her fingers slippery. She was able to ig-nore the pain for the most part, and her grunts and groans and occasional moans seemed al-most of pleasure.

In his office below, Conway had found his box of .38 shells, also buried beneath manuscripts, and he opened the box and began to methodi-cally load the weapon. This was how he had de-cided to pay off the woman he'd hired to kidnap and murder his niece, who still had to die.

He did not dislike the child—she was difficult to dislike—but her tragic death made an irresis-tible plot twist, further guaranteeing a best-seller, and besides, he would have his own children, someday, with Beth, who he genuinely loved. He didn't need to raise the child of some fucking sociopath.

His biggest challenge would be disposing of the body of the blond woman he'd hired to por-tray Mrs. Sterling.

As Conway was loading another round into the .38, Mrs. Sterling was withdrawing a bullet-shaped object from the flesh on her forearm. Like a sword from its scabbard, the blood-stained pel-let came, and the flesh sealed up behind it, and Mrs. Sterling's relieved sigh might have come from the slit in her flesh, closing its little mouth.

She held the tube of silicon up before her, be-tween her thumb and forefinger, and looked at the blood-smeared rod almost curiously; then she sneered and let out a tiny laugh of contempt that this pathetic little object might have caused her so much grief, and that anyone would imagine that such an insignificant piece of nothing could ever really stop the likes of her.

She rose, somewhat unsteadily, but moved quickly to the bathroom and found in a drawer by the sink an oversize Band-Aid to cover the small gash, which was not bleeding much, nor aching either. As she applied the bandage, she was breathing heavily, her chest heaving almost orgasmically as blood surged through her, her own blood, untainted by medical tampering, and after several dizzy moments, the face before her, gentle, peaceful, seemed to transform into something no less lovely, yet hard and very cold.

She looked in the mirror and saw herself. Her eyes tightened and she nodded at her image, as if agreeing with the woman in the mirror about what would happen next, or perhaps acknowledging an old friend noticed in a crowd; she wore only the faintest sneering smile as she tugged the white sleeve over the bandaged arm, smoothed her clothing, ran a hand over her hair, patting it in place, a professional woman checking herself before an important appointment.

Downstairs, Paul Conway—moving slowly, because as he loaded the weapon, he was in a sense writing, or at least plotting, a new ending for his story—snapped the .38 shut and rose to his feet. When he turned, she was sitting on his desk.

Mrs. Sterling.

Radiant in white, like a beautiful nurse, her hair icily golden, her well-shaped, sleekly nyloned, high-heeled legs crossed, she leaned on one arm, the other draped casually across her lap. He hadn't heard her come down the stairs; hadn't sensed her presence at all. Now, as if she had materialized, here she was, sitting on his desk beside the greenly glowing computer monitor whose screen was littered with his words. Perched on that desk, she was like a good-looking secretary in the days before sexual harassment became an issue.

She sat gazing at him, but it was not the sort of docile expression he would have expected from her these days; it was a face cloaked in confidence, heightened by a quietly mad gleam in the china-blue eyes.

"Where have you been?" Conway demanded gently. "Beth's out looking for you—we thought you'd taken Jessica Ann . . . is she with you?"

Mrs. Sterling said nothing, a smile forming faintly.

"The police are looking for you," Conway told her. "We better—"

"I heard you on the phone," she said matter-of-factly. "I know you've been framing me. I would have known sooner, if it hadn't been for *this*. . . ."

She held up the bloodstained implant, just long enough for him to see; then she flicked it over her shoulder, like a spent cigarette.

"You don't understand," Conway said reasonably. "I'm involved in a sting operation. Let me explain. . . ."

She slipped down from the desk, a hand behind her, and moved toward him slowly, but in the small space it didn't take long to close the distance as she said, "I wish I had time to listen. You really are an imaginative writer. But I have to help my daughter. . . ."

As she neared him, circling, he moved with her, a bull following the matador's lead. The faces in the pulp paintings seemed to watch them, waiting for this pair to join their deadly ballet of betrayal, lust, and death.

"This isn't the ending I had in mind," Conway said, and he raised the .38 and pointed it at her. "But I think I can make it play. . . ."

"You know," she said casually, as if this were a country club cocktail-party conversation, still slowly circling, not a bit concerned by the weapon in Conway's hand, "you may find it harder to actually kill someone than to just write about it . . . or hire someone to do it. . . ."

Then her casual tone hardened.

"It takes a special kind of person," she said, "to take a life."

And she swung her hand out from behind her back with sudden, swift savagery, a hand that clutched the dagger-shaped letter opener that had been presented him as an honor, only she presented it by slamming it deep into his side.

Conway's mouth dropped open in surprise and agony, and the gun flew from his fingers and landed with a clunk on the nearby desk, chipping the Sherlock Holmes mug. This was not a killing blow. The female matador was only setting the stage for the deathblow.

Grabbing onto his T-shirt with one fist and grasping the hilt of the letter opener, which stuck out of his side like a handle designed for that purpose, she flung him with bullfighter grace as easily as she would a rag doll, a sideways toss toward his desk, where his head crashed into the computer monitor screen, shattering it, his words disappearing, the tube imploding as sparks flew and smoke streamed and the air cracked and crackled with the sounds of electricity and the smell of cooking meat.

She appraised the scene—Conway was not quite dead, apparently, his arms stroking the air like a drowning swimmer, but he soon would be. Calmly she strode to the desk, checking her watch (Conway had promised his assassin he would meet her in half an hour), and discovered the notepad where Conway had scribbled, *Old Mill Park*. She knew where that was; that was easy. Conway was still floundering, twitching and shimmying, head buried within the jagged-glass mouth of the smoking monitor tube, dancing to the *zzzzzzzzzzsst* of electricity. She smirked at him humorlessly, wishing he'd have the courtesy to die and be done with it.

Then she noticed the .38 on the desk where Conway had flung it when she stabbed him. She picked it up, hefted it; the cool steel of the weapon felt good against her flesh, natural—this was not unlike the gun she used to own, the one she'd shot that bastard Mark Jeffries with.

She tossed Conway one last smirking, derisive glance—men were such idiots—and she walked up the stairs, not rushing, methodical, composed.

A mother on a mission.

Finally Conway lay slumped over his desk, his charred head deep within the monitor; the sparks, the pops, the cracks, the crackles were over. The author lay smoldering amidst his awards, surrounded by framed book covers—nearest him, *The Mommy Murders*—with the only true-crime books in his future to be written by other authors, with himself as the villain.

Right now, all that remained was wispy smoke and silence and the smell of scorched flesh.

And a small, bloodstained silicon pellet on the floor, forgotten.

Chapter Twenty-six

Jessica Ann woke up groaning, groggy, in the backseat of a strange car. She was still wearing her hot pink pajamas—short-sleeved top and knee-length shorts—although next to her on the seat, oddly, was a small stack of her clothes, as if someone had laid them out for her, to wear on a trip. Her white tennies were on top of the folded T-shirt and jeans.

Sounds of birds and not too distant rushing water—and the blur of green out the windows that met her eyes as she lay, propped up on her elbows, on the seat—told her the car was parked outside, somewhere, maybe in the country. Her mouth thick with a foul medicinal taste, her eyelids heavy, her muscles aching, her movements sluggish, slow, feeling like an insect in a spider's web, Jessica Ann sat up.

And saw the blond woman out the rear window, pacing over by some trees.

Jessica Ann ducked down, suddenly alert, her body functioning with precision; then she peeked out.

The woman had hair like Mommy's, the same golden twin arcs, and she was about the same size as Mommy, with a similar slender, shapely figure, ensconced in a white blouse and leopard-pattern culottes. She wore dark designer sunglasses, as Jessica Ann had seen Mommy do frequently, and she was smoking—a habit Mommy hid from her daughter but which her daughter was well aware Mommy had.

But this was not Mommy.

Jessica Ann could not fathom why, but she immediately knew this was a fake Mommy, a false Mommy, a bad Mommy designed to get her real Mommy in trouble again. Despite her dire situation, Jessica Ann experienced a surge of joy, having her opinion confirmed: She'd been right. Mommy indeed had been innocent of these murders.

The girl also knew, instantly, that she was next on the bad Mommy's list.

Ducking way down, snugging on her tennies, the child considered her options. She recognized where she was—this was the Old Mill Park and on a gloriously sunny perfect spring day; she'd been here many times, as had most everybody in

Ferndale. She knew at once that the blond woman had driven the car deep into the park, to this fairly remote graveled area; and she also knew that across the grounds, beyond the Old Mill, was a road that connected to highway 22.

The blond woman in the leopard culottes sucked on her cigarette as she paced, blowing dragon smoke out her nose, checking her watch, obviously irritated, obviously waiting for someone who was overdue.

But the woman was a good fifty feet from the car, and when in her pacing her captor turned her back to the red Sunbird, Jessica Ann quietly, cautiously, opened the rear door on the other side of the vehicle.

And slipped out, and slipped away.

The girl ran over a bluff and down the mowed grass of a steep hill, through golden sunlight, toward the trees. The sound of rushing water—the stream and dam by the mill—increased in volume as she ran, whispering to her, beckoning to her, leading her to a safe haven.

Jessica Ann's head start was short-lived, however, as when the blond woman in her pacing turned toward the car, she immediately saw the back door standing open.

Her pretty mouth peeled back in a snarl, she spat, "Shit!" pitched her cigarette, and perked her ears. She could hear the sound of the child's footsteps over the noise of the waterfall; as if a starter's pistol had fired, the blond woman took off running over that same bluff, and saw the bouncing blond hair and the hot pink pajamas disappearing into the trees.

Now Jessica Ann was in the green darkness of forest, hoping she hadn't been seen, dodging trees, cutting through high grass, pawing branches out of her way, her shoes snapping twigs.

But soon she could hear the blond woman behind her, moving through the same obstructions, the rustle of grass and leaves, the crack of wood underfoot. Her fear was her fuel, and she ran into sunshine, emerging from the trees to find herself running along the edge of the precipitous drop-off by the stream, the sound of rushing water running along with her, her companion.

Finally fatigue caught up with her, before the blond woman could, and the girl paused by an open-air chapel, leaning hands on knees near the stone benches, panting as a modernistic metal cross threw its cool blue shadow across her pink pajamas. Across the stream, the towering dark brown wooden clapboard three-storied rustic structure of the Old Mill rose like a great old church, the morning light shimmering on the water's surface. The peaceful, pastoral, picture-postcard beauty of it taunted the girl, but the rushing water urged her on, and she began to run again, slower, but running, as behind her the blond woman came charging out of the trees.

Up ahead was the wood-and-steel footbridge, and Jessica Ann took a shortcut down a rocky slope, every tiptoe movement a possible misstep that could send her careening down the rugged drop-off into the water. She threw a look back, despite the danger, and saw the blond woman coming, running past the outdoor chapel with a steady, fist-clenched gait, her face set in a hard frown.

Jessica Ann dashed across the footbridge, the ancient gray wooden slat floor trembling, the steel structure groaning and whining, and she was tiring again; it was too far to the road and to the highway after that. The Old Mill was off to the right and perhaps the blond woman was far enough behind her that Jessica Ann could, without being seen, cut over and slip inside the building and hide; the blond woman might assume the girl had taken the path up the hill to the road. . . .

So Jessica Ann, slowing, almost stumbling, trotted across the vast lawn of the Old Mill, a local tourist attraction she had visited with her school when she was in Mrs. Withers's class. But the sign on the door said CLOSED TO THE PUBLIC and there was a latch for a padlock; no padlock, though.

The girl opened the door and shut it behind her, moving quickly through the first floor, which was lighted only by streaks of sunlight finding their way, like swords in a magician's box, through what few windows weren't boarded up. She found herself in a rustic, open-beamed chamber where a giant wooden wheel loomed, part of an antiquated machinery that included other smaller wheels and strange gears and belts and pulleys.

This place hadn't seemed so weird on a school trip; but now grotesque shapes and twisted shadows transformed the 150-year-old structure into a carnival spookhouse. Turning in a terrified pirouette, the girl looked around her for a place to hide. Then she heard the blond woman at the door, and turned and ran down a passageway between a wall and an assembly of bulky wooden gears, feet echoing on the wooden floor.

The blond woman had not seen the girl enter the building, but Jessica Ann had unknowingly shut the door so hard it bounced back open; so, ajar, the door had attracted the blond woman's attention as she exited the mouth of the wood-and-steel footbridge, and soon she was pausing at the entrance to toss away her Ray Bans before entering, smug in her knowledge that the kid was at last cornered.

Jessica Ann found the stairwell and scurried up to the second floor, but the blond woman's footsteps reverberated through the building behind her, and the girl ran up another flight, her feet clattering up, each small footstep a gunshot, alerting her pursuer.

On the third, final, and darkest floor of the Old Mill, Jessica Ann again turned in helpless circles, finding nothing but more strange wooden machinery, wheels within wheels, big funnels, empty bins, boarded-up windows, and unfriendly walls, and then she bumped into something, crying, "Uh!"

But it was only a support beam, and as she whirled in relief, she saw the blond woman coming around the corner.

"Thanks for running," the blond woman said. Her upper lip was back and her teeth were showing; she was pretty, almost as pretty as Mommy, but there was something animal in her expression.

Jessica Ann backed up.

The blond woman was holding something; she whipped her hand around and a nasty blade jumped into sight, like a sharp silver tooth, glinting in a stray shaft of sunlight, the blade winking at her.

"Please," Jessica Ann whimpered, backing up some more.

The blond woman was advancing, and it was as if the knife in her hand was pulling her forward.

"I wondered if killing a kid would kinda . . . get to me," she said, more to herself than to Jessica Ann. "But you causin' me this much trouble . . . helps."

The girl's hands covered her mouth, her words escaping through her fingers: "Oh, please . . . no . . . no. . . ."

The blond woman continued her steady advance, saying, "Your uncle said I should strangle you . . . to make it look more like your mommy did it. . . ."

Her feet still backpedaling, her mind desperately trying to absorb the bizarre revelation that her loving uncle was part of this, Jessica Ann's hands fell from her mouth into a prayerful, pleading gesture, and she shook her head, saying nothing, her tearful eyes begging for mercy.

"... but it's just not my style," the blond woman said, closing in.

The girl bumped against the wall; its splintery surface scraped through her pajama top. Backed up, at a dead end, it was like she was in the junkyard again ... but in the junkyard, the real Mommy had spared her life; this bad Mommy would not. Weeping, the child began to pray, closing her eyes as the silver blade rose above her.

Why don't you pick on somebody your own size?"

The blond woman spun around, the knife flashing harmlessly above the head of Jessica Ann, whose eyes popped open at the sound of the familiar voice—*Mommy's voice*—and then there she was, all in white, like an angel, the good Mommy, rounding the corner, her high heels echoing, in no rush, a gun in her hand, but held almost casually, down at her side.

The blond woman grabbed Jessica Ann and pulled her into a short passageway between a bin and a wall that led into an open chamber, where only a few shafts of sunlight entered.

"Mommy!" Jessica Ann cried.

Mommy emerged from the passageway and

advanced toward them, slowly, steadily, her demeanor serene, even regal, her white suit glowing in the darkness.

"You know," Mommy said conversationally, "imitation's the sincerest form of plagiarism."

And with the faintest smile, Mommy raised the hand with the gun in it, pointing the revolver at the blond woman (and Jessica Ann).

"Mommy!" Jessica Ann cried.

The blond woman had Jessica Ann in front of her, the cold edge of the knife blade at the girl's throat.

"I'm walking out of here," the blond woman said coldly, but Jessica Ann could tell she was nervous. "You keep your distance, maybe the kid keeps breathing."

"Let her go," Mommy said reasonably, "and I'll let you go. . . . I have nothing against you."

"Nothin' against me?" the blond woman asked, yanking Jessica Ann back; the girl clutched the arm of the hand that held the knife, trying to pull it away, but the sharp blade remained pressed to her throat.

"Mommy!" Jessica Ann cried. "Help me!"

But Mommy was seemingly ignoring Jessica Ann, her eyes coolly locked on her daughter's captor.

"I know you're just a working girl," Mommy said matter-of-factly. Her eyebrows raised. "Oh . . . by the way—you're out of a job. I'm afraid I punched your meal ticket."

The blond woman's eyes widened, but she said

nothing. The two murderous women seemed to have nothing left to say to each other. They stood, in a classic Mexican standoff, staring each other down. Jessica Ann continued to struggle for seconds that seemed an eternity, and finally took control of the situation herself, sinking her teeth into her captor's forearm, biting down hard.

The blond woman howled in pain, jerking her arm reflexively away from Jessica Ann, who slipped from the woman's grasp, scurrying to safety, ducking behind a partial wall, around which she fearfully peeked.

The two women still faced each other—one with a gun, one with a knife. Mommy was smiling at the blond woman, a small, knowing smile, and the blond woman's eyes quivered in fear.

And Mommy fired the gun.

The bullet caught the blond woman in the shoulder, almost knocking her down, but she recovered enough to fling the knife, a savage overhand thrust.

The knife caught Mommy in the chest, near her left shoulder; it shook her, but she did not lose her footing.

"Mommy!" Jessica Ann gasped.

Knife hilt jutting from between her chest and shoulder, Mommy only smiled and, with quiet sarcasm, said, "Ow."

The blond woman, frozen in the half crouch of the knife-thrower, looked at Mommy with wide, terrified eyes, mouth open, the professional, master of her murderous craft that she was, suddenly realizing she was no match for a born killer, a true artist.

And Mommy, grimacing in contempt, fired again.

The shot caught the blond woman in the chest, flinging her backward, hard, into a boarded-up window behind her, and she burst through that window in a splintering explosion of wood, and was dead before she made her three-story journey to the cement dam below. Jessica Ann, in her hiding place, could hear the splat of the body, and covered her mouth in horror.

And relief.

Mommy, hilt of the knife protruding from between her chest and shoulder, stumbled to the now open window, gun in hand. Jessica Ann joined her mother there, and they gazed down at the dead woman in the leopard-print culottes, her white blouse stained with two red blossoms, a pool of spreading blood beneath her painting the gray cement crimson even as sunshine painted the corpse golden, while the water rushed over the dam.

Mommy heaved a sigh and lay the gun on the window ledge. Jessica Ann guided her mother gently away from the window and over to a small bench by the wall; Mommy groaned with pain as her daughter sat her down. Then Jessica Ann sat beside her mother, who was breathing hard, and took one of her mother's hands in one of hers, and slipped her other arm around Mommy, who nestled her head against her daughter's shoulder.

They were that way for several long seconds before the girl broke the silence.

"Who's your best friend?" Jessica Ann asked her mommy.

Mommy looked at her with surprise. ". . . You are."

"Who loves you more than anything on God's green earth?"

"Y-you do," Mommy smiled, her eyes wet.

Then the child began to rock her mother, comfortingly, staring straight ahead as outside the distant cry of police sirens drew nearer.

Chapter Twenty-seven

At the round table in the kitchenette of her Wesley House room, Mrs. Sterling sat—left arm in a sling, wearing a white blouse and the pink skirt of her suit, its jacket over the back of the chair—and was attended by her guest, Sergeant Max Anderson of the Ferndale police. He stood at her side, filling her cup from the Mr. Coffee pitcher. Just behind the woman, over the couch, hung a charming amateur oil painting of the Old Mill out at the state park, a tranquil landscape which lacked only the smashed-on-the-cement dead body that the cops had found waiting for them not so long ago, at that scenic spot.

Sighing, still standing, Anderson—dapper in a light green shirt with floral tie and suspenders—said, "Her name was Glenna Cole. Chicago girl.

Conway interviewed her for his contract-killer book, *Conversations with Killers*."

"Ah," she said, and it was unclear whether this was a response to what he'd said, or a small sound of pleasure at the taste of the coffee she'd just sipped.

Anderson placed the Mr. Coffee on a pot holder on the table and sat adjacent to her; they had traded chairs since his last visit—he was now sitting where she had been when he had grabbed her arm to check to see if she'd tampered with her implant.

"We're just beginning to dig into this," Anderson said, filling his own coffee cup; he was chewing gum. "But it appears Conway and Glenna Cole went to rather elaborate lengths to set you up."

"Really?" She seemed barely interested.

The detective pressed on, nonetheless. "We believe Conway, under an assumed name and with false credentials, rented Cole a Sunbird like the one you were driving. And in Cole's apartment, we found clothing identical to various things you were known to have worn before your arrest for the Mark Patterson homicide. They matched up with photos of you in Conway's *Mommy Murders* book, in fact."

She smiled sweetly, sipping her coffee. "That's nice," she said.

He looked at her, incredulous. *"Nice?"*

She shrugged. "I'm happy for you, Sergeant—tying up all these loose ends."

Anderson studied the perfectly composed woman, then asked, "How's your sister doing?"

"She's home," Mrs. Sterling said, her expression properly concerned, "but under sedation. Such an awful shock . . ."

"It may get worse. There's a possibility her husband and his pet contract killer were . . . romantically involved."

Mrs. Sterling didn't seem to hear that, saying brightly, "Beth thinks she's up to attending Jessica Ann's skating competition next weekend."

"Is she able to look after your daughter, in her stressed-out condition?"

Mrs. Sterling frowned mildly, shook her head, no. "Not really. And steps are being taken."

"Such as?"

"Well, I'm going to be moving in shortly."

"No kidding?"

Mrs. Sterling nodded. "In light of what's happened, my attorney has arranged for the restraining order to be lifted." She glanced around the plaster-walled, glorified cubicle, wearing a rather glazed smile. "I'll be getting out of this place very soon."

The media loved Mrs. Sterling now. She had saved her daughter; she had survived a plot to frame her for crimes she did not commit, which had opened up speculation that her original murder conviction might have been an injustice. And she was the poster child for mental health—proof that the new experimental antipsychotic drug was effective. She had received a supportive letter from the governor, and had heard from every major talk show in the country, with the exception of *Jenny Rivers*.

Even her cold-blooded murder of Conway (and that's what Anderson considered it to be, though in this case the homicide seemed justifiable) had been dismissed by the politically ambitious county attorney as self-defense. Prosecuting a mother for defending her daughter would be a very unpopular thing to do.

"New implant in place?" Anderson asked.

"Oh, yes," she said, and she touched his hand. She had a cool touch, but warmth flowed into him; the china-blue eyes sent subtle messages that made his tongue thick. He suddenly understood how all those men had gotten themselves into trouble in this lovely woman's arms.

"I've had some good news that may interest you," he said.

"Oh?"

"My former partner is making some progress."

"Lieutenant March?"

Anderson nodded. "He's regaining some movement. He may be out of that wheelchair within months."

"Good for him."

If there was sarcasm in her tone, he wasn't enough of a detective to search it out.

"Guess I owe you an apology," he said, removing his gum and tearing off a corner of paper napkin to wrap it in.

"No need."

He tossed the gum over his shoulder, snagging the wastebasket behind him. "Of course, even your doctor admitted something to me. . . ."

That seemed to alarm her.

He arched an eyebrow. "That last killing—Jolene Jones? That really did kinda fit your MO."

She smiled in apparent relief, not the response Anderson had expected to his thinly veiled accusation of murder.

But the detective had no way of knowing that Mrs. Sterling had been wondering if Price had revealed their affair; another murder accusation, more or less, was no big thing.

Her smile turned mischievous, and she shrugged a tiny shrug, saying, "I understood you'd cleared all those murders off the books."

He was pouring himself coffee now. "Yeah, uh, that was the county attorney's decision. But, you know, really only Jolene Jones herself could've identified her killer.

Mrs. Sterling frowned in what seemed to be concern, but there was something faintly mocking in her tone as she said, "Such a pity you can't ask her. . . . Could I have some more coffee, Sergeant?"

Anderson smirked, shook his head, said, "Sure," and poured her another cup. She raised it to him in a little toast, and Anderson shrugged and lifted his cup in a gesture of defeat, and a kind of salute to a worthy adversary. She had won.

This time.

Chapter Twenty-eight

The stands of the Ferndale Sports Center were packed, and applause rang through the vast skating rink, creating an unpleasantly metallic, machine gun–like echo, but none of the warmly attired spectators in the chilly arena seemed to mind. They were, after all, applauding their own children and grandchildren, nieces and nephews, as the winners of the afternoon skating competition were honored.

Olga, the wife of the late Matt Sharp, several months pregnant but not showing, was gliding by the latest group of six, with a flourish of a gesture, presenting the winners from the beginning skaters class. Three girls stood on the ice, while another trio took up the tiers of the three-leveled blue presentation platform. On the central, highest level stood Jessica Ann, golden hair ponytailed back, pretty and proud in a little red skating dress.

Jessica Ann was surprised she had won; the girl next to her, Heather Hahn, a tall, slender, pretty Korean girl adopted by a prominent local family, was an impressively athletic skater and had presented a more difficult routine than Jessica Ann, who was unaware of the extent of her own gracefulness and showmanship.

Many family friends were in the stands, including Mommy's attorney, Neal Ekhardt, and Mommy's psychiatrist, Dr. Price, whose son had won a medal today; the doctor was sitting with his pretty wife, not far behind Mommy and Aunt Beth. He seemed to be sneaking an occasional look at his patient.

Mommy looked beautiful in the red sweater with the black-leaf pattern; her hair was in a full, feminine style, gently curled at the ends, framing her classically lovely features like a golden halo. Her smile was dazzling as she applauded enthusiastically.

Jessica Ann ventured a tiny wave to her mommy, who waved back, then straightened herself with a familiar gesture, reminding her daughter to stand up straight. *Posture!*

Next to Mommy in the stands was Aunt Beth, who looked awful. Jessica Ann was pleased her aunt had decided to come today, but the girl was worried about her. Aunt Beth had hardly spoken since any of this had happened. Mostly what she had done was lock herself in the bedroom she used to share with Uncle Paul, and the sound of weeping would creep out from behind the closed door sometimes.

There had been no funeral for Uncle Paul, just a graveside service that Mommy and Jessica Ann did not attend (at Aunt Beth's request); from out of town, Beth and Mommy's younger sister Cindy had come, and stayed in the Conway house a while—their brother, Steven, had come for the graveside service, but just stayed overnight.

Now Mommy had moved into the Conway home, taking over the guest bedroom, and was already running the household while Aunt Beth, who was on a lot of medication, walked around zombie-like, when she walked at all.

The gold medal on its ribbon was placed over Jessica Ann's head by Olga, and the girl beamed at the crowd.

Sitting in the stands, in a black sweater and jeans, her usually lovely brown hair an unsightly tangle, her face devoid of makeup, her eyes deep and dark-circled, Beth applauded numbly, like a trained seal.

Her sister leaned in next to her, conspiratorially.

"I was afraid they were going to give first place to that little Asian girl," Mrs. Sterling said, working her voice up over the applause. "Just to be politically correct."

Beth said nothing, applauding in slow motion.

Mrs. Sterling faced forward again, stiffening. "They're lucky they did the right thing," she said coldly.

Slowly, Beth turned to look at her radiant sister, who was smiling the dazzling smile, bursting with pride for her little girl, covering her heart with her hand, sending her daughter a message of unconditional love.

And Beth, her eyes wide, her face blank, studied her sister for a very long time, feeling a chill that was not entirely due to the skating rink.

Jessica Ann's mother noticed neither her sister nor the cold.

DRAWN TO THE GRAVE
MARY ANN MITCHELL

"A tight, taut dark fantasy with surprising plot twists and a lot of spooky atmosphere."
—Ed Gorman

Beverly thinks that she has found something special with Carl, until she realizes that he has stolen from her. But he doesn't just steal her money and her property—he steals her very life. Suddenly she is helpless and alone, able only to watch in growing despair as her flesh begins to decay and each day transforms her more and more into a corpse—a corpse without the release of death.

But Beverly is not truly alone, for Carl is always nearby, watching her and waiting. He knows that soon he will need another unknowing victim, another beautiful woman he can seduce...and destroy. And when lovely young Megan walks into his web, he knows he has found his next lover. For what can possibly go wrong with his plan, a plan he has practiced to perfection so many times before?

_____4290-8 $4.99 US/$5.99 CAN

Dorchester Publishing Co., Inc.
P.O. Box 6640
Wayne, PA 19087-8640

Please add $1.75 for shipping and handling for the first book and $.50 for each book thereafter. NY, NYC, and PA residents, please add appropriate sales tax. No cash, stamps, or C.O.D.s. All orders shipped within 6 weeks via postal service book rate. Canadian orders require $2.00 extra postage and must be paid in U.S. dollars through a U.S. banking facility.

Name_____

Address_____

City_____ State_____ Zip_____

I have enclosed $_____ in payment for the checked book(s).

Payment <u>must</u> accompany all orders. ☐ Please send a free catalog.

SHADOWS

Kimberly Rangel

WHERE TERROR RULES...

In the distant past, in a far-off land, the spell is cast, damning the family to an eternity of blood hunger. Over countless centuries, in the dark of night, they are doomed to assume the shape of savage beasts, deadly black panthers driven by a maddening fever to quench their unspeakable thirst. Then Selene DeMarco finds herself the last female of her line, and she has to mate with a descendent of the man who has plunged her family into the endless agony.

_4054-9 $4.99 US/$5.99 CAN

Dorchester Publishing Co., Inc.
P.O. Box 6640
Wayne, PA 19087-8640

Please add $1.75 for shipping and handling for the first book and $.50 for each book thereafter. NY, NYC, and PA residents, please add appropriate sales tax. No cash, stamps, or C.O.D.s. All orders shipped within 6 weeks via postal service book rate. Canadian orders require $2.00 extra postage and must be paid in U.S. dollars through a U.S. banking facility.

Name_____
Address_____
City_____State_____Zip_____
I have enclosed $_____ in payment for the checked book(s).
Payment <u>must</u> accompany all orders. ☐ Please send a free catalog.

A KILLING PACE
LES WHITTEN

"Gritty, realistic, and tough!"
—*Philadelphia Inquirer*

For George Fraser, dealing and double-dealing is a way of life. But with the body count around him rising higher, he decides he wants out of the espionage business. As a favor for an old friend, Fraser agrees to take on one last job: just running some automatic weapons—no big deal. Then the assignment falls apart, and Fraser is caught in the sights of terrorists determined to see him dead. Suddenly, Fraser is on a harrowing chase that takes him from the mean streets of Philadelphia to the treacherous canals of Venice. He is just one man against a vicious cartel—a man who can stop countless deaths and mass destruction if he can keep up a killing pace.

_4017-4 $4.99 US/$6.99 CAN

Dorchester Publishing Co., Inc.
P.O. Box 6640
Wayne, PA 19087-8640

Please add $1.75 for shipping and handling for the first book and $.50 for each book thereafter. NY, NYC, and PA residents, please add appropriate sales tax. No cash, stamps, or C.O.D.s. All orders shipped within 6 weeks via postal service book rate. Canadian orders require $2.00 extra postage and must be paid in U.S. dollars through a U.S. banking facility.

Name_____

Address_____

City_____ State_____ Zip_____

I have enclosed $_____ in payment for the checked book(s).

Payment <u>must</u> accompany all orders. ☐ Please send a free catalog.

CHARLES WILSON
NIGHTWATCHER

"A striking book. Quite an achievement."
—*Los Angeles Times*

The staff of the state hospital for the criminally insane in Davis County, Mississippi, has seen a lot in their time—but nothing like the savage killing of Judith Salter, one of their nurses. And with three escaped inmates on the loose, there is no telling which of them is the butcher—or who the next victim will be. Even worse, as the danger and terror grow apace, the only eyewitness to the nurse's death—a psychopathic mass murderer—begins to reveal a fearsome agenda of his own.

___4275-4 $4.99 US/$5.99 CAN

Dorchester Publishing Co., Inc.
P.O. Box 6640
Wayne, PA 19087-8640

Please add $1.75 for shipping and handling for the first book and $.50 for each book thereafter. NY, NYC, and PA residents, please add appropriate sales tax. No cash, stamps, or C.O.D.s. All orders shipped within 6 weeks via postal service book rate. Canadian orders require $2.00 extra postage and must be paid in U.S. dollars through a U.S. banking facility.

Name_____
Address_____
City_____ State_____ Zip_____
I have enclosed $_____ in payment for the checked book(s).
Payment <u>must</u> accompany all orders. ☐ Please send a free catalog.

Max Allan Collins

"Chilling!"—Lawrence Block, author of *Eight Million Ways to Die*

Meet Mommy. She's pretty, she's perfect. She's June Cleaver with a cleaver. And you don't want to deny her—or her daughter—anything. Because she only wants what's best for her little girl...and she's not about to let anyone get in her way. And if that means killing a few people, well isn't that what mommies are for?

"Mr Collins has an outwardly artless style that conceals a great deal of art."
—*The New York Times Book Review*

___4322-X $4.99 US/$5.99 CAN

Dorchester Publishing Co., Inc.
P.O. Box 6640
Wayne, PA 19087-8640

Please add $1.75 for shipping and handling for the first book and $.50 for each book thereafter. NY, NYC, and PA residents, please add appropriate sales tax. No cash, stamps, or C.O.D.s. All orders shipped within 6 weeks via postal service book rate. Canadian orders require $2.00 extra postage and must be paid in U.S. dollars through a U.S. banking facility.

Name_____
Address_____
City_____State_____Zip_____
I have enclosed $_____ in payment for the checked book(s).
Payment <u>must</u> accompany all orders. ❑ Please send a free catalog.

ATTENTION WESTERN CUSTOMERS!

SPECIAL
TOLL-FREE NUMBER
1-800-481-9191

Call Monday through Friday
12 noon to 10 p.m.
Eastern Time
Get a free catalogue,
join the Western Book Club,
and order books using your
Visa, MasterCard,
or Discover®

Leisure
Books

MOMMY'S LITTLE HELPERS

This book has a somewhat unusual derivation. It is a sequel to my novel *Mommy,* which was an expansion of my short story of the same name (published in the Warner Books anthology *Fear Itself* edited by Jeff Gelb) and the screenplay based on that story.

Mommy was produced in 1994, an independent feature that I wrote, directed and produced after raising the funds to do so in my hometown, Muscatine, Iowa. Against considerable odds, *Mommy* proved a cultish success upon its 1995 release to video and cable.

Encouraged, we gathered most of the same cast and crew in 1996 and created a sequel, *Mommy's Day* (called *Mommy 2: Mommy's Day* in the home video market). As I write this, it's difficult to know if the second film will do as well as the first, but the predominantly favorable critical reaction indicates that at least some people agree that we came up with the rare sequel that is superior to the original.

The book in your hands is not a "novelization," although that ignoble form is one at which I'm fairly adept. *Mommy's Day* expands not only on my screenplay but also on an unpublished, unfinished prose version that was begun months prior to my shooting the feature. My intention had been to create *Mommy's Day* as a short story prior to making it as a movie; when I got to about page 70, however, I realized I wasn't writing a short story, but a novel, and set it aside. The first third or so of the book, then, is an expansion/reworking of that material, which predated the film.

Nonetheless, elements of the film crept into the novel, and I would like to thank the following actors whose performances followed me into the writing of *Mommy's Day:* Michael Cornelison, Gary Sandy, Paul Petersen, Brinke Stevens, Mickey Spillane, Larry Coven, Del Close, Pamela Cecil, Todd Eastland, Sarah Jane Miller, Arlen Dean Snyder, Marian Wald, Carol Gorman, Tom Castillo, and of course Mommy and Jessica Ann—that is, Patty McCormack and Rachel Lemieux.

Lyrics from two songs featured in the film are excerpted in this novel; thank you to Paul Thomas for permission to quote from "If Life Was Fair." (Passages from my song, "Shockabilly," also appear here.)

And I would like to acknowledge a few of my filmmaking collaborators: Phil Dingeldein, Steve Henke, Greg Ballard, Bob Hurst, Rico Lowry and of course my wife, Barb Collins. Others deserve mention but space doesn't allow (buy or rent *Mommy 2: Mommy's Day* for the complete listing).

Finally, thanks to editor Don D'Auria for buying *Mommy* and requesting this sequel, and to my agent, Dominick Abel, for letting me do it.

**The cult movies written and directed
by Max Allan Collins!
"THE BAD SEED grown up...chilling!"
—Leonard Maltin**

MOMMY (1995) —★★★, New York Daily News. *Patty McCormack, Jason Miller, Majel Barrett, Brinke Stevens, Mickey Spillane and Rachel Lemieux as Jessica Ann.* Widescreen Collector's Edition featuring Patty McCormack interview, trailer, still gallery. VHS video #2150, $14.95.

MOMMY 2: MOMMY'S DAY (1997) —★★★, New York Daily News. *Patty McCormack, Paul Petersen, Gary Sandy, Brinke Stevens, Mickey Spillane and Rachel Lemieux as Jessica Ann.* Widescreen Collector's Edition featuring Patty McCormack interview, trailer, still gallery. VHS video #2160, $14.95.

From your video dealer or order direct from:
VCI Home Video, 11333 East 60th Place, Tulsa, OK 74146.
Or Call 1-800-331-4077.
$4.50 shipping/handling for one, $.50 per additional tape.

LASER DISC WIDESCREEN COLLECTOR'S EDITIONS are $49.95. From your favorite laser dealer or The Roan Group, 361 River Sound Village, Hayesville, NC 28904. Or Call 1-704-389-0597.

Also: *MOMMY* audiobooks read by Patty McCormack
MOMMY $16.95 ($4.50 shipping/handling)
MOMMY'S DAY $16.95 ($4.50 shipping/handling)
At fine book and music stores or available direct from SUNSET PRODUCTIONS, 369 Montezuma #416, Santa Fe, NM 87501. Or Call 1-800-829-5723.